William Kotzwinkle is a writer who enjoyed a large underground following before achieving international success with his widely-acclaimed novelization of the film *E.T. the Extra-Terrestrial*. He is the author of several works of fiction including *Fata Morgana*, *The Fan Man*, *Doctor Rat* and *Elephant Bangs Train*. His deeply moving novella, *Swimmer in the Secret Sea*, was the winner of the 1975 O. Henry Award. He lived, with his wife (also an author), for several years in Canada and now lives in the United States of America.

Also by William Kotzwinkle

THE MIDNIGHT EXAMINER

and published by Black Swan

The Hot Jazz Trio
William Kotzwinkle

Illustrated by
Joe Servello

BLACK SWAN

THE HOT JAZZ TRIO
A BLACK SWAN BOOK 0 552 99440 5

First publication in Great Britain

PRINTING HISTORY
Black Swan edition published 1991

This book is set in 11/12pt Mallard
by Busby The Printers Ltd, Exeter

Black Swan Books are published by Transworld Publishers
Ltd, 61-63 Uxbridge Road, Ealing, London W5 5SA, in
Australia by Transworld Publishers (Australia) Pty. Ltd,
15-23 Helles Avenue, Moorebank, NSW 2170, and in New
Zealand by Transworld Publishers (N.Z.) Ltd, Cnr Moselle
and Waipareira Avenues, Henderson, Auckland.

Made and printed in Great Britain by
Cox & Wyman Ltd, Reading, Berks.

*Django
Reinhardt
Played
The Blues*

Smoke curled around the little bare stage where Django Reinhardt played his guitar. A cigarette dangled from his lip, and a bottle of wine stood beside his stool, half gone. The black hand of Argos the bass player thumped out the rhythm behind him, and the American expatriate saxophonist played his American expatriate saxophone, thinking to himself, *Already the music is joining itself to a far-off time.*

'Illusion has entered,' said Argos, nodding toward the door of the café, where LeBlanc the magician had come in, his eyes immediately seeking the stage.

LeBlanc came to the edge of it and stood there; a bright handkerchief appeared in his hands and with it he signaled the waiter. A drink was brought to him, and he paid for it by drawing a franc note out of the hat of a woman seated nearby. The woman noticed nothing, the waiter accepted the franc note, and LeBlanc drank in a single swallow as Django ended the set. 'Well,' said Django, 'what is the matter? You look like you've swallowed a goldfish.'

'I've lost Loli.'

'Your assistant?'

'I put her into the Vanishing Lady Box—' LeBlanc wiped his brow nervously. '—and she vanished.'

'So?'

'She truly vanished. The box is meant to conceal the performer, not devour her. I don't wish to reveal the secret of the trick, of course.'

'Of course,' said Django, politely.

'But she has gone. She disappeared from the face

7

of the earth—' LeBlanc looked at his watch. '—about twenty minutes ago, during my last show.'

'You have searched the box?'

'Don't be an idiot. It's empty, and Loli is gone.'

'Then you'd better have another drink,' said Django.

An empty table, the worst one in the house, was reserved for the musicians. Argos and the American expatriate saxophonist joined Django and LeBlanc, and they contemplated Loli's fate.

'She's deceived you,' said Argos.

'No, I took her from a wretched existence and made her a star.'

'Being sawn in half is not stardom,' said Django.

'It is better than some jobs,' said the American expatriate saxophonist.

'The point is,' said LeBlanc, 'she's gone and I'm responsible. It was my box she vanished from.'

Django squinted over his cigarette. 'Do you have any clues?'

'None.'

The musicians and LeBlanc turned the dilemma over many times and swirled the ice in their glass. The master of ceremonies, with a nod toward Django, took the stage. 'Messieurs, mesdames, once again, the Hot Jazz Trio.'

Django turned to LeBlanc. 'After closing . . . '

At the corner of rue de Varennes and boulevard des Invalides is an old mansion called the Hôtel Biron. The garden is luxurious and muffles the sounds of the street with a veil of reeds and twined branches. Django led the way up moss-covered steps, across a carpet of forget-me-nots, and through a small portico to a set of French doors. He knocked. When no answer came, Django pushed gently and entered. Within lay a man on a small studio bed, eyes glazed, an opium lamp smoldering beside him on a low table. His long index finger lifted in greeting. 'My Gypsy,' said Jean Cocteau softly.

'I would interrupt your dreaming only with a matter of urgency.'

'Life is the interruption,' said Cocteau. He gestured and the Hot Jazz Trio sat, while LeBlanc paced nervously and Django described Loli's disappearance.

Cocteau's lips formed a thin smile, and he looked out the window toward the garden. Django remembered a deep song of Andalusia, one he'd not thought of in years, about a girl at the bottom of the sea. LeBlanc continued his nervous pacing, absentmindedly snapped an ace out of his sleeve. Cocteau's eyes, like those of a reptile, gazed through the smoke of his lamp.

They entered by the stage door into a darkened hall. LeBlanc led the way to his dressing room, where the Vanishing Lady Box was stored. 'I swear you to secrecy,' he said as they entered.

'Of course,' said Cocteau. He traced his fingers along the box's rivets, the real ones and the fake, these being simply the heads of rivets, with no shafts attached. Behind the main chamber was a false one, into which the assistant could step, invisible to the audience.

'In every way, it is an excellent box.'

'But tonight,' said Cocteau, stepping into it, 'it has eaten your assistant.'

He put himself into the mystery chamber and had LeBlanc seal it. In the perfect darkness of the illusion, he felt the hands of nothingness caress him. How much had Loli learned while assisting with this act?

A guitar stood in the corner of the dressing room; it was an old instrument with worn frets and battered face. Django picked it up and played the song of the girl at the bottom of the sea, and Argos felt a disturbance of melancholy, a conjunction of hour, place, and the Gypsy's hand. He leaned back against the peeling white plaster wall of the room, closed his eyes, and saw a young woman – was it Loli? – walking down a boulevard lit by pearls, and her walk was slow, as if the fog surrounding her held her step.

'She owed me money,' said LeBlanc, 'but that is no reason to disappear, my terms are not unreasonable.' He opened a trunk, took out a slip of paper. 'Her IOU,' he said, holding it up, then making it disappear into the palm of his hand.

Cocteau, still wrapped in darkness, laid his head against the mahogany frame of the box. Its false door is not as false as one might think . . .

Django played, and the American expatriate saxophonist stepped out of the room and wandered onto the shadowy stage of the empty club. Django's melancholy guitar followed, faintly sounding, as if heard through the walls of time. Once again the American expatriate saxophonist felt how their music was dropping into the past, its quality changing even as it was played, and fading into that which is mistakenly called memory.

Babette, a girl of the streets, stopped them as they were leaving the club. 'You have closed the place, messieurs. And still you aren't tired? Has one of you a match?'

Her cigarette was lit by a flame from LeBlanc's fingertips, as if his fingernails were sulphurous. 'You are a hot customer,' she said.

'We're looking for Loli,' said LeBlanc. 'She used to work around here.'

'She went off with a knife thrower.'

'*Pardon*,' said LeBlanc, 'she went off with a magician.' He brought his heels together with a click.

'What do you need Loli for,' said the girl. She turned slowly, hands on her hips. 'You can throw knives at me.'

'Yes,' said LeBlanc with an approving nod. 'I may be needing a new assistant.'

They left her in her pool of lamplight, as Cocteau's shadow slipped along the pavement, bending itself over stoops and railings, moving with its own understanding of events on rue de Clichy. It was wily, cautious, flexible as shadows are, dropped down through the drains, moved along the curb, was intimate with the street's

11

facade. Only in profile was its mouth revealed, but its words were vapor of another dimension. Did it know where Loli was?

LeBlanc produced a cigarette from his cuff, with no trace of the match that had lit it; smoke trailed over his fingertips as he brought the gold-tipped weed to his lips. He turned to Argos. 'Assistants should not vanish into thin air, not from a box as expensive as that one.' Impatient plumes of smoke swirled from his nostrils.

'Yes,' said Argos, 'one expects objects to behave.' But he knew that his bass fiddle had a secret rendez-vous, that she had escaped the club after closing time.

Cocteau's gaze was recasting the street into a thorough-fare of dreams whose perspectives led to cities of jeweled insects, eyes winking in the distance; two pipes ago he had supped with the Spider Prince.

'Where did you acquire your box, LeBlanc?'

They followed boulevard Haussmann to rue Taitbout and then to boulevard des Italiens. The theatrical supply shop was dark, but a streetlamp cast a faint glow on an assortment of costumes and masks suspended in a gloom that gave them life.

'A stuffy place,' said LeBlanc, 'and disorganized. I found the box on its side, under a pile of old playscripts.'

Cocteau nodded, as he studied the costumes in the gloom. A woman's sleeve was extended in the dark toward a limp, headless Pierrot. At the portal was a suit of mail, a helmet – and beyond this guard, the floating wisps of a mad king's wig. From creatures such as these, enchantment could be expected.

'As you see,' said LeBlanc, 'it is a harmless jumble shop.'

They walked on. There was, upon the boulevard at that hour, one café still lit. Its crowd had thinned, but the scattered chairs, abandoned any which way, showed it had been a night of the usual argument and debate, resolved in drunken gesture. Cocteau moved slowly, as through water. Before him in the rippling depths was a blue-black face – native of a tropic shore and wandering here without compass at the end of night; a small kit bag was hung on the back of the sailor's chair. The blue-black seaman looked up and saw, instead of Cocteau's face, a parrot, bright-beaked, with sharp, curious eyes. This momentary apparition was replaced by Cocteau's boney countenance, but the eyes of the bird remained. The sailor nodded and Cocteau sat down, motioning LeBlanc to sit beside him. The Hot Jazz Trio was already heading toward the bar.

The seaman's own eyes had become slits. 'Well?' he asked, moving his head just slightly to the side, as he maintained his study of the strange Parisian bird before him.

Cocteau's eyes flashed upon the sailor whom chance had placed in his path, as chance has vowed to do. 'We're searching for a girl who's lost her way.'

'I did not mislead her.' The dark-skinned sailor smiled.

He's worn a pearl through his nose, observed LeBlanc, studying the perfectly round hole in the sailor's flaring nostril.

She was part of a magic act,' said Cocteau. 'This is Monsieur LeBlanc, *Illusionniste Extraordinaire.*'

LeBlanc's fingers rippled, and a rose appeared within them and vanished again with a twist of his wrist. The sailor smiled, his white teeth brilliantly gleaming, one of them filed to a sharp point. His gaze returned to Cocteau. 'And where do you think this girl of yours has gone?'

'Perhaps she is lost in a poem,' said Cocteau. 'But one thing is certain, she has vanished from this—' He knocked his fist on the irrefutable reality suggested by tabletops.

'And what have I got to do with it?' asked the seaman.

'I know the skin of Tierra del Fuego,' said Cocteau. 'You men of blue are masters of many spells.'

13

Again the sailor saw the face of a parrot cover Cocteau's countenance. 'You have much to do with birds.' The sailor reached behind him to his bag. He unlaced the side with a yank of the slipknot and laid back the flap. He brought out a small brown sponge, the size of a human heart. He set it on the table before them and tapped the sponge lightly with the tip of his finger. 'Squeeze it.'

Cocteau picked the brown sponge up and placed it in the palm of his hand. Its dark pores were not eyes, but the sponge saw.

'Squeeze,' repeated the sailor.

Cocteau's long fingers closed upon the sponge. A woman's voice came from the interior, out through the pores. He felt it running over his fingers like watery silk.

'*I've been abducted,*' said the voice, floating disembodied in the air.

'We are here to help you, mademoiselle,' said Cocteau, opening his grip.

'Give me that—' LeBlanc grabbed the sponge and shouted at it, as if it were a telephone. 'Loli, you little tramp, where are you?'

'Squeeze it,' smiled the sailor of Tierra del Fuego, lowering his sharp fang over his lip, enjoying the familiar contour of its edge. He nodded at the sponge.

LeBlanc squeezed it, and Loli's voice came out through the pores. '*Help me, LeBlanc.*'

LeBlanc stared at the sponge, then at the sailor. 'Monsieur, may I ask you what my assistant is doing in your sponge?'

'Perhaps she is bathing,' said the sailor.

Cocteau laid a finger on LeBlanc's sleeve. 'The sponge has only absorbed her cry.' He put his lips to the pores of the sponge and whispered into it, slowly and distinctly, then closed his fingers once again around it.

Loli's voice came through less distinctly than before, her watery words trailing off, dissolving, evaporating, and then the sponge was silent. The sailor extended his palm. Cocteau placed the sponge in it. 'Thank you.'

'Not at all.' The sailor put the sponge into his bag and laced it up.

LeBlanc leaned across the table toward him. 'That's a first-class act. Care to sell it?'

The seaman smiled again. 'I would like to oblige you, *may suhr*, for I see you are a clever man. But I merely carry this for another.' He patted the side of the bag. 'It belongs to him and I cannot sell it without his consent.'

'Where might I find him then?' asked LeBlanc. 'I'm prepared to spend a bit. A talking sponge would fill the gap for me, until I can find another assistant for my Vanishing Box.' LeBlanc's fingers again moved swiftly, colored blossoms dancing between them, then vanishing back into his sleeve. 'So? Where does the owner of the talking sponge hang out?'

'At the bottom of the sea, *may suhr*.' The sailor rose slowly from the table, and put the bag over his shoulder. His eyes met Cocteau's, and Cocteau pitched forward with the sensation of falling from a window. But in fact he had not moved, as he realized a moment later, finding himself still upright in his chair.

'If you change your mind,' called LeBlanc, 'my card.' A small white rectangle appeared at the tips of the magician's fingers, and the sailor smiled, taking it into his own. LeBlanc nodded. 'I'll give you five thousand francs for your Talking Sponge.'

The black sailor, adjusting his sack, moved a step away from the table. 'That is a lot of money, *may suhr*.' His voice, a mellow syrup, came as if from the depths of a floating barrel, and then he bobbed on, between the rows of half-turned chairs, and out through the door.

'So,' said LeBlanc, 'who was he?'

'Who indeed,' murmured Cocteau softly, as he watched the man's shadow pass the window and vanish.

They met the following afternoon, in the Luxembourg Gardens. LeBlanc found Cocteau on a bench, the poet's eyes closed; had LeBlanc been able to look in a certain way, he would have noticed the entities of the breeze

16

who'd been attracted to this soft statue in the park, motionless, concentrated in the pool of fantasy, with a fine spray falling on him from the fountain of dreaming.

LeBlanc spoke, his voice banishing the fountain's discourse. 'I thought you might not be here.'

Cocteau opened his eyes. 'I am here, LeBlanc.' He smiled at the magician, who was already nervously pacing by the bench.

'The police came to my club, asking about Loli. What could I tell them? That she'd vanished in my box, in front of a hundred people? I had to skate around, improvise. I'm sure they now suspect me.'

'Well, you are suspicious, LeBlanc.' Cocteau stood, and his arm came out from under his cape, indicating the route they must take across the park.

'I? Suspicious? I'm a hardworking artist.' LeBlanc swung a silver-headed cane, skimming it lightly over the grass. 'But bad publicity could hurt me. Club owners are conservative beasts. They don't like their magicians under police surveillance.'

'It is an opportunity for you to learn more about your art,' said Cocteau.

'You, of course, have the mind of a fish. I don't say it's not useful, this underwater approach, but . . . '

'Your father was the son on Leonide LeBlanc, was he not?'

'He had that distinction, yes.'

'Your grandmother could vanish at will from men's eyes, into a cloud of roses.'

'All I've inherited from that family is insomnia,' said LeBlanc. 'It led me to seek night work.'

Cocteau's shadow mixed with those of the trees, falling on their greater shapes, freeing itself each time like a wandering man-root, ancient and unencumbered. And did it know where Loli was? But how does one question one's shadow? reflected Cocteau. And who casts whom, that is the first question. Does this impudent silhouette believe that it creates me? It is the myth of shadows, that they cast behind them a gross and ponderous double known as man.

'I can make things appear, disappear,' said LeBlanc, 'make people believe they see things that aren't there, but I'm not like you. I don't wander around submerged.' He glanced sideways at Cocteau. An exceedingly odd person, with oriental habits; but clever, there was no denying that, if you enjoyed the mentation of fish.

LeBlanc was in his less formal afternoon wear, but all his clothes were tailored for tricks; a coin appeared in his fingers as he scratched behind his ear; a handkerchief three yards long waited in his sleeve. 'You're sure Loli's not dead?'

'Not dead.'

'Inconsiderate of her, all this, don't you think?'

'She can't help what has happened.'

'She asked too many questions for an assistant.' LeBlanc drew a lit cigarette from his vest and put it, smoking, to his lips. 'And she frequently tried to upstage me.'

Ahead of them, in a dense growth of vines and hedge, a single sunflower had been planted by a bird and had blossomed. Its green velvet stalk should have been twisted toward the sun, but instead the great golden bloom was facing the path. Had it turned toward them?

Cocteau approached the sunflower slowly, as toward a wild beast that might bolt. Its luxurious petals quivered at their tips as if in fear of attracting anyone to their secret. He stepped closer, a faint trembling in his own limbs, a disturbance in his liver, perhaps, or some other human frailty aggravated by the spirit of opium.

Monsieur Cocteau, said Loli.

Her hair was an arrangement of golden petals, her face a mass of yellow seedpods; her eyes blinked slowly in the center of the blossom, lids heavy, as if waking from sleep. *Monsieur Cocteau* . . .

Her lips were opening seedpods, whispering. *I have no wish to be a sunflower, I'm just a magician's assistant.*

'I'm coming to help you, Loli. But I must find the doorway first.'

18

'To whom are you speaking, Cocteau?' LeBlanc pulled the edge of his handkerchief out nervously, three lengths of red, blue, and gold silk fluttering; the sunflower accepted the gesture, and LeBlanc found himself staring into Loli's face, hung upon the stalk. 'Loli, darling Loli, what is this?'

I'm lost, LeBlanc. I took a wrong turn in your box.

'Don't worry, we shall water you, tend you, dig you up and bring you home. LeBlanc's talking sunflower, a major attraction, Loli, you'll be a headliner.'

Au revoir, messieurs . . .

Loli blinked and vanished. The sunflower turned, back toward the sun slowly, its audience with the human world ended; LeBlanc gazed regretfully at the plant. 'That would have made me the toast of Montmartre.' He snapped his handkerchief, and the long length of silk vanished.

They wandered, and streets blended one into the other. 'It eludes common sense, Cocteau.'

'She is lost in another world, LeBlanc. You cannot use common sense.'

'She's lost in a *box*, my dear fellow. A big stupid mahogany box. I can think of nothing more common.'

'Your box grew tired of being so dull. Perhaps it had grown to adore Loli.'

LeBlanc uttered a snort of contempt; an India rubber ball appeared in his palm and rolled up to his elbow. He twitched that joint, the ball rose into the air, and vanished. Cocteau was nodding to himself, for he'd felt the brute personality of the box and its coarse passion for Loli.

'I've always considered it a box without wit, Cocteau, though well crafted. It has the smoothest-working hinges I've ever seen. Where are we going, by the way?'

'Somewhere in this city, there is another entranceway to the world into which Loli has gone.'

'And what world is that?'

But Cocteau didn't answer, for whatever word he might use to describe it would deceive them. It was the world of shadows, and the thought of flowers, and convulsive moments.

He says nothing, reflected LeBlanc. *Does he know? Am I wasting my time with this philosopher? Ladies and gentlemen, the coin is mesmerized* . . . He practiced as they walked, and they walked far.

Cafés are sometimes the gates. Cocteau and LeBlanc drank, smoked, waited. 'Who made the box, LeBlanc, do you know?'

'It came from Hamburg. You saw that it was old.'

'Yes,' said Cocteau, 'its hinges are well worn.' And the patina of the wood is somber now, after how many thousand magic nights. It absorbed the mystification of its audiences, nourished itself, grew bold . . .

LeBlanc was dealing card hands on the table, spreads that would turn into runs of spades or clubs, with an ace that kept popping up everywhere and then vanished with a snap behind his fingers. He did this automatically, as he talked. 'Yes, old, from Hamburg. Fine brass ornamentation, not the kind of stuff you can easily get these days. I had Loli polish it. She had that box looking like something.'

Cocteau stood up, moved suddenly toward the door, LeBlanc hurrying after him. The magician caught a glimpse of someone moving into a narrow lane opposite the café. 'It hugs the walls . . .' Cocteau pointed, and LeBlanc saw an enormous serpent writhing ahead of them, down the stone corridor between two tenements. Cocteau started to run, and LeBlanc followed. The serpent undulated with a soft brushing sound along the stones, then dove into a crack in the wall; as the two men reached it, only the tail was visible, and it wriggled out of sight with a last slithering rasp of its scales. LeBlanc stared at Cocteau. Cocteau nodded toward the end of the passage, adjacent to the quay and the river. 'It will find its way to the water.'

'A moment, please. I saw a man enter this passage, not a serpent. What is going on, Cocteau?'

'In every city,' said Cocteau softly, 'there are those who are not quite right, not altogether human.'

LeBlanc looked toward the windows of the tenement building. 'And what of the people in this house, who have a serpent crawling through their cellar?'

'They will hear its rustling,' said Cocteau, continuing on down the narrow lane toward the quay.

'My god, it was big enough to swallow a man.' LeBlanc shook his head slowly and turned back to look at the crack in the stone through which the serpent had passed. 'If you have an explanation for this, I insist on hearing it.'

'We don't want to disturb it with explanations.'

'Disturb it? I should like to hit it over the head with a meat-ax.'

They stepped together onto the quay, the last light of afternoon falling now upon the bookstalls and the river. LeBlanc felt unbalanced, as if the sidewalk might suddenly shudder beneath his feet. Cocteau felt the city itself shifting. But then, he told himself, Paris is not unaccustomed to this. No, she merely shrugs when her basilisks act up.

'Someday a child will be walking in that alley,' said LeBlanc.

They continued along the quay, as the evening settled in around them, and figures in the distance, upon the bridges, grew indistinct. LeBlanc was still feeling the tremor of the serpent. 'I have a popular magic act—' He gave his nose a nervous tweak. '—I was never interested in monstrosities.'

Did I imagine, reflected Cocteau, that its tail, just at the tip, was silk?

LeBlanc, with a sudden start, perceived that their shadows were *falling the wrong way*, along the quay. 'Cocteau!' He turned to the poet, but as if turning with him, the shadows righted themselves.

Cocteau hailed a cab, instructed the driver to go where he liked, and then sat back, deep in the seat. LeBlanc watched out the other window. He had a show

at nine, and should have eaten, rested, rehearsed a new assistant. Instead . . .

The cab took them across the river, continued on: rue du Havre, avenue de Villiers, to the Place Malesherbes, where Cocteau stopped the cab, climbed out, led them on, past the handsome private residences of the area. In front of a sixteenth-century mansion they stopped, gazing in at the gardens, where bronze figures gazed back. 'Dumas the Elder,' read LeBlanc.

'The Grief of Orpheus,' said Cocteau.

They walked, their footsteps like blue oil, soft, reflective, and their shadows quite as slippery, knowing more. Night was falling as they reached the Square des Batignolles and circled it slowly. The twin fountains held their tongues, but the bronze figure of Circe followed them with a turn of her bewitching head. LeBlanc dropped an ace and was startled by his clumsiness. 'Cocteau, we are being followed, I do not know by whom.' He retrieved the playing card from a pool of water on the sidewalk, and looked back along the way they'd come. But the square was empty.

'Yes, followed,' said Cocteau, and nodded toward the ragged background of the square, which was advancing on them. But as soon as he pointed, the background withdrew, as had the misplaced shadows when spied by LeBlanc. 'It is timid,' said Cocteau. 'Yet it is only waiting for an opportunity.'

LeBlanc gazed uneasily over his shoulder at the immensity of that which seemed to stalk them now. 'What has this to do with the box?'

The box has friends, reflected Cocteau. When inanimate things rise up against us . . .

'Reason underlies the magician's art,' said LeBlanc. 'I am not accustomed to being followed by city skylines.'

Cocteau returned to his room, his scarlet cloaked bed, his pipe. 'Where have you gone, Loli?' His cat washed herself, and his pile of books and journals were starlit. He rose from the bed, walked to the large blackboard that leaned against the wall. He drew a box, within a box, within a box, and within that box the figure of a man dancing.

LeBlanc had difficulty on stage, his cards refusing to obey, his handkerchiefs undisciplined. He was still faster than his nightclub audience, but he was not the Great LeBlanc tonight.

' . . . and now, ladies and gentlemen, the Chinese Ribbon, which I shall cut, like so – only to have it restored, like so – here, please examine it yourself.' He threw the bright ribbon into the audience. It fluttered over a ringside table, fell into charming hands, which could discern no seam, no tear, no cut, of course. LeBlanc told the young lady to keep the ribbon as a memento of this magic night.

He bowed, had the feeling that something in hibernation was waking in the room, a tortoise or a crocodile, something ancient opening cold eyes. He quickly scanned the audience; no crocodile sat at a table, tail around a chair leg. Rather it seemed the room itself was this crocodile, jaws wide apart, with lamplit teeth. It was the ragged horizon coming for him again, an immensity of shadow. He threw up a hand to protect himself, then saw, at that same moment, Cocteau, entering the club. The immensity withdrew, and LeBlanc brought a bouquet from his sleeve to mask the gesture of fear he'd made.

Cocteau took a seat near the stage, his table lit by a small beaded lamp. He smiled at LeBlanc, and LeBlanc was flooded by more uncanny feelings – concerning this shape of a man before him, this poet, this sleepwalker. Cocteau seemed to be aglow, but not with halo or aura or internal light; he glowed in his infinite possibilities. LeBlanc felt a pressure building in the room.

The ragged outline, the menace of shadow, had returned with renewed force. Cocteau felt not a crocodile's mouth but a trick handkerchief like LeBlanc's, one without end, pulled from the sleeve of night and falling around him. He struggled to free himself, for though one may desire adventure, to suffocate . . . ?

LeBlanc saw Cocteau rise, he seemed to swim, and then, quite suddenly, he wasn't there. And it seemed, not as though he'd vanished, but as if he'd never been there at all, for the table that the waiter had set at his entrance was bare as before. The jaws of the crocodile had swallowed him, and swallowed the piece of time he'd inhabited.

LeBlanc looked down, saw in his hand the Chinese Ribbon, which should have been in the audience; saw in his other hand the scissors with which he was about to cut it. He performed the trick, threw the ribbon, and was seasick as he saw its waving tail and saw the girl in the front row catch it with exactly the motion she'd caught it before.

He ended the act and walked backstage to his dressing room. He entered, walked over to his mirror, gazed into it. 'Now Cocteau is gone too.' He loosened his bow tie. 'Will the police be on me for that, as well?' He threw his silk hat down, then sagged into a chair. From a gilt cage, his pigeons cooed to him, but he was not consoled. He turned toward his box.

'You swine.' He rapped the box with his cane. 'What perversity are you practicing on that innocent girl?'

The box seemed to shine, with pride. LeBlanc drew back, in loathing. 'And now Cocteau. His absence will certainly be remarked upon. And with whom was he last seen? LeBlanc the magician. The one whose assistant . . . ? Yes, odd, isn't it.' In a burst of anger, he hurled his cane at the box. It struck, clattered to the floor.

But Master, said the box, *I did not swallow Cocteau.*

'No? Then who did?'

Cocteau emerged in the soul space of the inanimate. Here, boxes came and went, thumping. He sensed a guide beside him, turned, and was greeted by a length of silk streaked with color. A silver belt encircled its waist, and its arms were defined by slight twists in the silk. It wrapped an end of itself around Cocteau's wrist.

'Where is Loli?'

The silk shape formed a mouth crease, and spoke in

25

a whisper of soft, indistinct rustling. The tug on Cocteau's arm was insistent, and he followed.

The gloomy landscape was lit as if by a distant bulb of dim wattage concealed behind a paper bag. The ground was polished wood of fantastic grain depicting human scenes, greatly distorted, the perceptions a box might have absorbed into itself. Cocteau followed the tugging arm of silk. 'Was it you who brought me here?' he asked, and the silken crease answered with its soft whisper and wrapped another length of itself around his wrist.

Boxes thumped around him, seemed not to notice him until they came close, and then they rocked back and forth; they were all ponderously heavy and capable of crushing him flat. He edged carefully around them, with the voice of the silk still rustling near his ear.

'Cocteau is gone.' LeBlanc sat down at the table of the Hot Jazz Trio.

'Gone? Where?' Django peered at him through a curl of cigarette smoke.

'He has vanished like Loli. Into thin air.' LeBlanc related the circumstances of the poet's disappearance.

'And so, once again,' said Django, 'you look like you've swallowed a goldfish.'

'I'm dropping aces,' said LeBlanc. 'I'm losing my fine edge.'

Argos looked at the rattled magician, who nevertheless was causing a coin to walk over the backs of his fingers. 'You're next, LeBlanc.'

'No! LeBlanc never disappears! Only his assistants.'

'Most certainly next,' intoned Argos.

'Don't tease LeBlanc.' said Django, 'or pigeons will come out his sleeve and crap on your instrument.'

The American expatriate saxophonist felt an inexplicable anguish pass through him and recognized the dead end of night, when it seems the air is made of stone, where nothing gives and there is no response. *What is this life I've been believing in?* he asked himself. He

26

walked to the stage, picked up his saxophone, and the seizure passed, but a note of caution had been struck.

LeBlanc rose from the table. 'I must return for my next act.'

'We'll come round,' said Django.

'I'm grateful, gentlemen. I have no friends among the other magicians. We're a spiteful lot.'

'Drink some hot wine,' said Argos. 'Have a custard.'

LeBlanc retreated back up the aisle through the tables, and the Hot Jazz Trio watched him go, but their thoughts were of Loli and Cocteau. 'In Gypsy caravans,' said Django, 'women disappear under mysterious circumstances, never to return, or if they do return, are changed forever.'

Cocteau was led to the encampment of the silken beings.

'*Enchanté – enchanté—*' He moved among them, and they touched him with their delicate appendages. He felt a discomforting atmospheric pressure, which bore upon his emotions as well; it was with difficulty that he reconstructed his reason for being here – to find Loli. He felt silken thoughts weaving with his own, erasing his memory, and he perceived that the nature of these beings was to seduce.

'I am searching for one who would be a stranger in your land, one like myself, who stumbled on the entranceway—'

They seemed not to listen, were too busy parading him through their camp. Lights appeared beyond them when they danced, shining through their bodies, but when they turned, there was nothing.

'That is why they call us veils,' said a voice by his side, and he turned, startled. A veil was speaking to him, a wrinkled fold moving in its face.

'You are surprised by my power of speech, but after all, I have lived in Paris.'

'Ah,' said Cocteau, 'and where would that have been?'

'I belonged to a vicomtesse. She wept in me.' The handkerchief paused, as if in thought. 'It explains my melancholy nature.'

'I am looking for Loli. She vanished into a magician's box.'

'These things occur.' The creature seemed to sigh into itself. 'But you will never find her.'

'But why not?'

'The brutish boxes have her, that is why. Surely you know they cannot be opened.'

Cocteau returned his gaze to the veils undulating before him, through which the soft lights shone. And the veil beside him, who spoke such excellent French, put a silken hand upon his thigh.

LeBlanc was in his dressing room, practicing a new rope trick; at first the ropes wouldn't obey, but LeBlanc knew that his fingers must be given time. He worked, and before his cigarette was finished he had the trick. '*Voilà!* And so, ladies and gentlemen, LeBlanc has once more traced that pathway which is faster than the eye. Watch, stare, try to see how – but you cannot.'

He chuckled to himself, enjoying the mystification that was his livelihood. But then, thoughts of Loli and Cocteau returned to trouble him. 'The police think I have hidden her body somewhere. Walled it up. But, officer, she stepped into my box and that was the last we saw of her. Tell us another one, Monsieur LeBlanc.' He ground his cigarette out and shook his head. 'My excellent magic show could find itself in exile. Pulling Polish pigeons out of a hat in Dogrobutchka. I, the toast of Paris.'

He stood, adjusted his bow tie, prepared for the next act. From outside in the club came the sounds of the dinner audience. They were applauding the team of naked jugglers; he passed them in the hallway, and they nodded indifferently at him as they walked by, bearing their hoops and balls. He touched his hat to them, as always, and swiveled his head to watch them continue down the hall to their dressing room door, which closed with a bang.

He walked into the wings of the tiny stage and waited there for his cue. The master of ceremonies was beyond

him in the spotlight, drunk, gesturing extravagantly. ' . . . and next, we have the Great LeBlanc, that celebrated magician whose last assistant vanished, ladies and gentlemen, without a trace, from inside his box. The police have been called in . . . '

The audience applauded enthusiastically, and LeBlanc reflected on the possibility of getting another assistant and having *her* disappear too. But could the box be depended on?

LeBlanc finished at midnight; he took his customary table by the kitchen and drank black coffee. A candle burned on the table before him. He stared at it, searching in his mind, as always, for some new trick. 'I could try a bullet-catching act. The noise is deafening, and the effect heroic.'

He looked up to see the Hot Jazz Trio crossing the club floor. 'Well,' said Django, 'how are your nerves holding out?'

'Sit down,' said LeBlanc.

They sat, Argos looking at the handful of customers who still remained, talking quietly at their tables. In this late hour, they were no longer figures in a nightclub crowd, but personalized bits of mood, their cigarette smoke and murmuring voices a kind of music that worked upon his soul. He listened, and absorbed the mystery, one part of which was the fact that he knew he would be the forgotten bass player, a black man in Paris, known to have played with Django. Will anyone suspect that Argos was bewitched?

'While we were playing tonight,' said the American expatriate saxophonist, 'I heard Cocteau's voice. He said he'd gotten involved with a piece of silk.'

'Just the kind of thing I was worried about,' said LeBlanc. 'The man's a notorious opium smoker and totally unreliable. I've hung around with silk for years.' He pulled a red length of it from his sleeve with a flourish. 'I know all about the fabric, and I appreciate its uses.' He blew out the candle and dropped the square of silk over it. 'But I've never been attracted to it sexually.'

He pulled the square of silk away, and where the candle had been, a bouquet of flowers now sprouted from the candle holder.

'And you say he vanished from the audience during your act?' asked Django.

'Into thin air, just like Loli. One moment he was seated at that table over there—' LeBlanc pointed. 'And the next moment he was gone.'

'He couldn't have just walked out?'

The magician's eyebrow arched. 'Nobody walks out on LeBlanc.'

'I see.' Django picked a flower from LeBlanc's bouquet, put it in the lapel of his jacket, and walked over to the table from which Cocteau had disappeared. It was an ordinary table, surrounded by ordinary chairs. The floor, the wall behind it, the ceiling above it – ordinary.

Well, he said to himself, this is certainly the ship that has got out of the bottle, isn't it.

'You'll find nothing at this table,' said LeBlanc. 'I've been watching it all evening, and it is in no way remarkable.' He brought a lit cigarette from behind the American expatriate saxophonist's ear and began puffing on it. 'Heat and mechanics, gentlemen, can make odd things happen in this world. The libation fire of the Romans would cause air to expand within their altar, which caused a certain contained liquid to flow, which then moved attached ropes and rods, and these would bring the doors of the altar mysteriously open. But this—' He lifted the chair, and set it down with a little bang. '—is a simple, and if I may say so, dumb chair.'

The Hot Jazz Trio and LeBlanc circled the table slowly, and it remained as it was, almost smugly, an indisputable bit of the common unwavering reality.

Cocteau lay in a silken embrace, the creature wrapped around him lightly at the ankles, and again at the wrist. The sensuous cloth creased into a mouth, whispering, 'Your hands are long and fine. I adore boniness.'

The silken being coiled gently around his torso. 'I am

31

spun by worms dreaming of their wings. My secrets are from their tiny meditations and the chatter of the loom. I am the veil called Bombyx.'

'An American doctor said I had the most depraved face he'd ever seen. But I've never been involved with a veil.'

I am searching for someone, thought Cocteau. But who? It is slipping from my mind. All is silk and my beautiful Bombyx.

'I know the trick of the Educated Fish, who can write Napoleon's name on a piece of paper, but I am at a loss in this business,' said LeBlanc.

'Do the statues come off their pedestals when nobody's looking?' asked Argos softly.

'I tell you what I think,' said LeBlanc. 'You can shave a donkey, and a moment later all his hair has returned. You can do wonders with sleight of hand. I think—' He paused, peering ahead of them up the dark street. '—there is some other magician who has come to Paris and is staging all this.'

'A greater magician than you, LeBlanc?' asked Django.

'I know it is hard to imagine. And of course the moment I meet him I will challenge him to a contest.' LeBlanc tapped his ebony cane on the sidewalk. 'He has the advantage over me now, because he is operating from behind the scenes.'

'And he stole Loli and Cocteau?'

'Covered them. They are under a cloth somewhere.'

Django looked at the other members of the Hot Jazz Trio. They shook their heads. 'Sorry, LeBlanc, we don't buy it.'

LeBlanc spun his cane. Fire shot out both ends of it, followed by roses, their petals dripping moisture. He clicked his heels, spun the cane again, and the roses vanished. 'Then I have no more to say.' He appeared miffed.

Django put his arm around LeBlanc's shoulder. 'We'll find Loli, wherever the hell she is.'

And the American expatriate saxophonist glimpsed

something from his childhood following him, something like music, which exists apart from men's thoughts about it. And he heard a piece of chamber music in his head. *That is Rossini's*, he said to himself and remembered having played it when he was a boy. But why now? And why this strange sensation of something being lowered onto his head, a sort of net, and the strains of Rossini growing louder?

'The penalty for taking the heavenly silkworms back to the dimension of earth is death.' Bombyx talked to Cocteau in a mulberry grove, where cocoons glowed in the leaves, a soft, nestled sheen – for each thread in the little wrapping was made of light.

'It is from these that you are made?' asked Cocteau, touching one of the cocoons.

'These are my progenitors,' said Bombyx.

Cocteau, connoisseur of narcosis, was suffused with well-being – except for a woman's voice, faintly calling, *Monsieur Cocteau, Monsieur Cocteau.*

He walked on with Bombyx, whose method of loco-motion was an upright slithering.

. . . I've been taken by the boxes, Monsieur Cocteau.

'Ah, Loli!' Cocteau snapped awake. 'Bombyx, you must help me.'

'I'm not made for battle,' said Bombyx. 'I'm for weeping, or wrapping around the hair.'

'The Vanishing Birdcage is a handsome contraption, and it works perfectly every time.' LeBlanc talked on as they walked the boulevards toward the dawn. 'It does not devour birds, never to release them again.'

'LeBlanc,' said Django, 'you've got to face something. We're dealing with supernatural forces.'

'The greatest of mediums, the Fox sisters themselves, were debunked. The spirit rappings heard in their homes were actually the sisters cracking their toe joints.' LeBlanc gestured with his cane, as if at an adversary in the dark. 'And I shall debunk the rascal who has done

this to me. The Great LeBlanc will not be toyed with. I'm beginning to see clearly on this matter. It will be but a short time and I'll have solved it.'

'Then you won't be needing us?' asked Argos.

'Please,' said LeBlanc, 'you are the Conjuror's Assistants.'

LeBlanc and the Hot Jazz Trio met the dawn in the square of St Sulpice. They were alone there in the dew. Argos, Django Reinhardt, and the American expatriate saxophonist sat on a bench, facing LeBlanc. The magician stood on the path before them, performing sleight of hand. His cane turned into an umbrella, he twirled it once, opened it, and a square of bright silk hung from the tip of every rib.

'Bravo, LeBlanc,' said Django sleepily, slumping down on the bench.

The umbrella spun once more and the silks flew off, uniting themselves into one large square of silk imprinted with a Chinese dragon. 'Now, gentlemen, watch carefully.'

LeBlanc twirled the large silk in the air over his head. It descended gently around him and covered him down to his shoes. A second later it collapsed to the ground, and LeBlanc was nowhere in sight.

Django came quickly off the bench, but then approached the square of silk cautiously. It lay flat on the ground. He tiptoed over and discreetly picked up one corner. 'LeBlanc?'

A banner, borne in the beak of a bird, fluttered by. The banner read LEBLANC IN THE LAND OF THE MAGICIANS.

LeBlanc gazed up at it, watching as the bird bore the banner away over the horizon. He turned, trying to reconnoiter. 'I've been magicked away. I, the Great LeBlanc.'

If word of it ever got out, he'd be ruined. But he felt he could trust the Hot Jazz Trio to say nothing. Meanwhile, there was no doubt whatever that somebody was trifling with him.

To his right was a magician's table, with a pitcher and two bowls. To his left was an elegant apparatus fitted out with dangling braided cords – a piece he recognized as the Ropes of Rangoon. Not wishing to touch another man's show, he wandered on.

The ground was covered with a worn wooden floor, which extended in all directions. 'Most peculiar,' remarked LeBlanc. It was as if the whole place were a stage. Plush clouds overhead were red and hung like the folds of a curtain, which moved along in pace with him, seeming to frame him continually before an unseen audience. The horizon glowed, as if from distant footlights.

A soft sound of silk being snapped came at his ear, and a moment later he was staring into the eyes of an English magician, made up as Oriental.

'I am Hop Sing Woo.'

He had a bullet hole in his chest, for which he apologized. 'Shot, you see. The pistol misfired on stage at the Admirals-Palast in Berlin.'

'Bullet-catching trick?'

'A lady friend,' replied Woo, 'filed down the screw that plugged the live chamber.'

'Angry with you?'

'Mad as a hornet.'

'One can't be too careful with women,' said LeBlanc. 'I'm here because of one. By the way—' He gazed around. '—what sort of place is this, anyway?'

'Hard to say,' said Sing Woo.

'Well, where's the exit door?'

'Some try the Orange Tree Transformation. Others use the Lady Seated in the Chair. You'll vanish all right, but to where?'

'To the park of St Sulpice in Paris, I should hope.'

'No guarantee,' said Sing Woo. 'What if you come out in a bug's ass?'

'Not what I had in mind,' said LeBlanc. 'Look here, Woo, I need your help. My assistant, Loli, was vanished out of Paris after months of arduous schooling in my unique routines. You know how hard it is to come up with a well-trained assistant.'

'Mine shot me to death, I know it well,' said Sing Woo.

'Well, there you are, a difficult business. So Loli has vanished, and I must find her. There's also a poet who disappeared, a drug fiend named Cocteau. We might try to find him too, though it's not strictly necessary.'

'In the words of Confucius – what's in it for me?'

'I'll give you, free of charge, my Trick of the Talking Pomeranian.'

'Don't sell me yesterday's newspapers, LeBlanc.'

'Very well, I'll throw in the Tray of Flaming Forms.'

'Generous, aren't we?'

'Those illusions were immensely popular in Dogrobutchka, my good man.'

Hop Sing Woo agreed to the arrangement, and the two magicians set off to look for Loli.

The Hot Jazz Trio caught some sleep, and then, after another night's playing, were back on the streets again. 'I want to buy some little candies,' said Django. He purchased a tinful of lavender drops, handed them around.

The American expatriate saxophonist had LeBlanc's dragon silk around his neck, which he tied in a loose cravat. 'If you ask me, silk is behind much that has happened.'

'I knew a woman called Silk,' said Argos, sucking a tiny heart-shaped candy, 'and she made a fool outta me.'

They returned to LeBlanc's club. The magician's dressing room was lit by a bare bulb. The Hot Jazz Trio poked around the collection of magic props – swords, knives, birdcages, top hats, flowers. The door opened behind them and Mignonne, the club singer, stepped in. 'What happened to LeBlanc tonight? I had to do five shows in a row. I'm exhausted.'

'LeBlanc was magicked away,' said Django. 'Disappeared under a silk scarf.'

'Silk sheets, you mean.' Mignonne sat down, crossed

37

her legs. 'He's with some girl, I'm sure, while I sing until I'm hoarse.'

'And now you're really ready to sing,' said Django. 'Now you're warmed up.'

Mignonne looked up at the Gypsy through half-closed lids. *This Django Reinhardt,* she thought to herself, *with his little mustache.*

She rose, swaying slightly as she gazed around the room. 'What a lot of junk. What's this box? Is it the one he uses in his act with Loli?'

Mignonne opened the door of the Vanishing Lady Box.

'Don't step inside that damn thing,' said Argos.

'Why not?' said Mignonne, who always did what she liked. She stepped inside the box and the door swung closed on her.

'But of course,' said Django, yanking open the door, 'she had to stick her nose inside, and now—'

'Farewell, Mignonne.'

The empty cabinet seemed to be smiling, as a gentleman might after a good cigar, and a mood of contentment emanated from it.

Django heard Mignonne inside his heart, singing one of her sultry songs, about a girl who walks all night thinking of a man. And he knew, quite suddenly, that she and he had something going. *But how can we dance if she is magicked?*

'Boys,' he said, 'I'm going in after her.'

He stepped inside the box, into the scent of Mignonne's perfume. It had its own magic, and wispy feminine arms twined round him, pulling him into the other dimension. But their power was fragile, and he felt only a shoulder going, then one leg, then half his head and torso.

When the Hot Jazz Trio opened the door, the remaining half of Django stepped out. A seam of flat black enclosed him all down the side. '*Mon dieu,*' said Django's half mouth. 'I've come unzipped.' His one eye stared frantically around.

'How can we take you anywhere in that condition?' asked Argos.

'Take me anywhere? You idiot, how can I play the guitar? *Mon dieu, mon dieu* . . .' He hopped around on one leg. 'This is the most uncomfortable arrangement conceivable . . . '

'We'll have to put this cloak over you.' The American expatriate saxophonist put LeBlanc's midnight blue cape around what was left of Django Reinhardt.

'Get a wheelbarrow,' said Django. 'I can't walk.'

'We'll carry you,' said Argos. 'We're the Hot Jazz Trio.'

'The Hot Jazz Duo and One-Half,' said Django. 'I'm screwed. I'm done for. All I can play is the tambourine.'

'We'll work something out.'

Django hopped toward the door. 'Let's get going, while it's still dark.'

'It must be a Gypsy curse.' They made a Boy Scout chair with their interlocked hands and carried Django out into the night.

The other half of Django was in the Land of Boxes, on a parquet floor that went forever. Standing beside him was Mignonne, peering at him suspiciously. 'Where's the rest of you?'

'In LeBlanc's dressing room.'

'A lot of good that will do us.'

'Look here, my girl,' said the Gypsy, 'I've just been sawed in half, and I'd appreciate a little tenderness.'

Mignonne put one hand on her hip. 'What is this place? Some filthy trick of LeBlanc's?'

The guitarist balanced himself on Mignonne's shoulder. 'Give me your arm, I'm tottering over.'

'I like a man who can stand on his own two feet.'

'If I had two feet I'd oblige you, but since I don't, would you spare me the indignity of having to hop around like a toad?'

Mignonne's arm slowly rose, index finger uncurling until it was pointed straight at the half of Django's nose that remained to him. 'Musicians are always taking advantage of me.'

'I do not call this an advantage.'

'I knew LeBlanc was a fiend.'

'If you'd have pulled harder you'd have all of me.'

'I don't want any of you.'

'I was under the impression that you cared.'

'You were wrong.'

Django sidled up to Mignonne, trying to give her the old Gypsy charm, though he had only half a mustache to work with. 'I like the way you sing that song of yours, about the woman who walks all night, thinking about a man.'

'She should have her head examined.'

Django flailed at the air, trying to stay upright. 'Must you stomp around so fast? Have pity on those less fortunate.'

'How do I know you aren't faking?'

'Faking?'

'I'm hungry.'

Django reached into his pocket. 'My heart, mademoiselle.'

Mignonne took the little lavender candy and popped it in her mouth. As the flavor of the heart drop broke upon her tongue, she heard Django's guitar inside her, playing a song she had sung as a child, in rue Danton, on a certain sunlit day. 'Gypsy, how do you come to know so much about me?'

'I'm just a bifurcated guitarist.'

'Don't play the backward fellow with me. It is well known that your guitar gets into a woman's memories and causes trouble.'

'I'm in no shape to cause any woman trouble.'

'Liar.'

'I lost half my ass trying to rescue you.'

'A fireman would have been more useful.'

'One was not available.'

Begining to enjoy Django's discomfort, Mignonne tapped him in the chest with one finger and crowded him as he stumbled backward. 'Jazz musicians are to blame for much that happens to young women.'

'I don't deny this.'

'What's going to happen to my career?'

'What has happened to my ass?' Django stared disconsolately downward.

'You have a following. People come from far away to hear Django Reinhardt.' Mignonne adjusted the thin shoulder strap of her camisole. 'I'm an unknown, and I can't afford to miss a show.'

'I'll have to be propped up by a clothes pole.' Django now tried to progress by twisting little motions of his one foot, but he tended to go sideways instead. 'I'll be renting a mechanical arm. Have you thought of that?'

'You'll scrape through.'

'I must lie down.'

'Don't try that fainting act on me.'

'Where did you learn your great compassion, Mignonne? I should like to know. It humbles me.'

She crossed her arms stubbornly over her breasts. 'My father was an organ grinder. I was his monkey.' She saw a shadow on the ground – her father's hunched form in his drooping coat and battered hat, passing the way a bird's shadow passes, swiftly. 'Papa and I worked neighborhoods like this where you couldn't make a dime. Where is everyone anyway? Where do people hang their wash?'

'These are the streets of Nod, Mignonne.' Django was getting an unbearable pain in the kneecap from his twisting shuffle, but self-pity kept him going. How in hell did this happen to me, he asked himself. You try to lead an exemplary life, and things foul you up anyway. 'There's no fighting it, Mignonne, I've been cursed.'

'Stop your sniveling.'

'Once, while having an innocent midnight smoke, I accidentally tossed a match in my wife's cooking oil and burned our wagon to the ground. It's all part of an evil pattern.'

'You should have been more careful.'

He could stand it no longer; he collapsed in a heap at Mignonne's feet, striking hard on the ground. He tapped it with his knuckles. 'Have you noticed it's made of wood?' He flopped over on his back like a fish. 'And the sky is painted on. I'm not one for nature, but this place could stand a bush or two.'

'I draw my strength from an audience.' Mignonne ignored the prostrate guitarist, her gaze still searching for that aged shadow of the street organist and the secret it held, but it had flown over the horizon, with the indifference of birds. 'Who can I sing to here?'

'Some might suggest you try and cheer a poor half-assed guitarist with a song. Remind him of better days.'

'It's no place for a singer. The acoustics are lousy.'

Django tried to rest his head on Mignonne's shoe tip. 'I knew a Gypsy woman with a voice like a crow, but she found her groove and I tell you, that was some croaking.'

A woman's hooded figure crossed the wooden plain in the distance. Django forced himself upright, trying to catch a better look, but the figure vanished. He turned to Mignonne. 'Who was that?'

'My future,' said Mignonne quietly.

'Then mine must be around here somewhere too.' And Django's music sounded on an old recording.

LeBlanc and Sing Woo walked along through the Land of the Magicians. The trees were fake, the sky was painted, and there were trapdoors everywhere. 'Tricky place,' said LeBlanc.

'You'll get used to it,' said Hop Sing Woo.

'I'll not be staying long.'

Hop Sing Woo pointed to a woman's scarf, floating in the air. 'Recognize it?'

LeBlanc grabbed it, examined it carefully. 'Cheap stuff. Not from my act.' He released it, and it continued on its way, fluttering like a butterfly searching for a flower.

LeBlanc looked around at the painted backdrop, which kept following them, always at the same distance. In the foreground a similar painted scene was hung, and it kept pace with them too. 'Any idea how big this place is?'

'No one knows,' said Sing Woo. 'You can see why.'

The two magicians continued along, over the wooden plain. LeBlanc saw a small white figure hopping along ahead of them. He pointed, but Hop Sing Woo shook his head. 'White rabbit. Lots of them around.'

LeBlanc nodded. 'Useful creatures. Ears for lifting out of hats. God created them that way for magicians.'

Hop Sing Woo maintained the lead, as if he had some clue to Loli's whereabouts. His short form, clad in Oriental costume, seemed the very essence of tenacity, until a trapdoor opened under him, swallowed him up, and then closed without a trace.

LeBlanc stood alone on the wooden plain. Another trapdoor opened up ahead and Woo climbed out, covered in cobwebs. LeBlanc rushed to his side. 'Are you all right, old man?'

Woo brushed the webs off his face. 'Have you enemies, LeBlanc?'

'Certainly. You know the jealousy that breeds in our profession.'

'And are you armed?'

'I've avoided pistol tricks. I mean, look what happened to you.' LeBlanc indicated the bullet hole in Sing Woo's chest.

The Hot Jazz Duo and One-Half moved cautiously along through the Parisian night, with Django wrapped in LeBlanc's cloak. 'I need a drink,' said the halved guitarist.

'You'll have to keep that cloak around you,' said Argos.

'Naturally,' snapped Django peevishly. 'Do you think I have some desire to appear publicly, sawed down the middle?'

They assisted him into a dark after-hours club and propped him up on a chair in a secluded corner, with his good side facing outward. 'Son of a bitch,' muttered Django as he teetered off the chair. 'I've only half an ass to balance on.' He slouched forward, supporting himself against the table.

In this fashion he waited for a drink, and when it came

his two colleagues had to prop him up while he drank it.

'I'll get to the bottom of this.'

'Sure you will,' said Argos. 'They can't do this to you for long.'

'I'll have to pluck the guitar with my teeth.'

'We'll arrange everything,' said the American expatriate saxophonist.

'What do you mean, you'll arrange everything?' Django slumped forward, drink sliding away from him. 'I've been sliced in two. What possible arrangement can be made?'

And the Hot Jazz Duo and One-Half pondered on this, deeply.

'You have a little act,' said Django morosely, 'you try to keep it going—'

'There are some blues, Django,' replied Argos. 'I've never heard the like.'

Django shifted uncomfortably in his chair. 'I don't say LeBlanc is to blame. But a magician should discipline his box.'

'We'll be playing this years from now,' said the American expatriate saxophonist.

'You'll be playing it,' said Django. 'I'll be selling pencils.'

'Have another drink.'

'No, I can't handle it. I'm plastered already.'

'You're not metabolizing,' said Argos.

'You have a medical degree?'

Picasso entered the café, as was his custom at this hour, the pockets of his ill-fitting suit filled with the bits of trash he collected on his excursions through the streets. Argos waved him over to them, lifted Django's cloak. Picasso nodded. 'Put him against the wall.'

Argos and the American expatriate saxophonist propped Django up, and Picasso went to work reconstructing the missing half of Django.

'Will it look like me?' asked Django nervously. 'My mustache is a delicate matter.'

Babette, the bird of the night, entered the café with a

colleague, Giselle, and the two women sat down with Argos and the American expatriate saxophonist, Babette peering critically at the work in progress. 'I wouldn't trust Picasso to stick me back together.'

'He puts eyes in the side of the head,' agreed Giselle.

'Picasso,' said Django, 'is this so?'

'Don't concern yourself,' said Argos. 'You're a museum piece.'

'I have no wish to see like a chicken,' said the Gypsy.

'Picasso,' called Babette, 'where are you going to put his little Django?'

Giselle, with a Gauloise stuck in the center of her mouth, and her own memories of Picasso from the days when the artist regularly visited the Belly of Paris in search of handlebars, crossed her legs, and adjusted the uneven hem of her homemade flowered skirt. 'If I was being rebuilt I'd ask for one yellow eye and a jewel in my lip.'

Django peered desperately through his one eye at Picasso. 'Just keep it simple, Pablo.'

'Don't move,' growled Picasso.

'Sorry.'

'Django,' said Giselle, 'I heard your music floating in the Passage Choiseul today . . . '

' . . . and I,' said Babette, 'at the market at Gare de Lyon.'

'Django's soul came apart,' explained the American expatriate saxophonist. 'It went in different directions.'

'I was buying two cauliflowers,' said Giselle, 'and they turned into roses. I was so moved I went and had my dog shampooed. Nobody plays like Django.'

'And we run into him now,' said Babette, 'up against the wall like a purse snatcher.'

'With his nose on his elbow.'

Picasso was working quickly with the bits of trash he'd collected, giving Django a pocket watch for an eye, a piece of licorice for a mustache.

'Django's music makes me feel I'm the moonlight,' said Giselle, who was just a little drunk, but it was the truth, she'd heard it floating down through the bars the night the police interned her at Saint-Lazare.

'Done!' Picasso stepped back. Argos and the American expatriate saxophonist stared at a secret Django they'd long suspected; looking at that pocket watch in Django's eye, they realized they'd seen it before, one night on the bandstand, when they'd played 'I Know That You Know' faster than anyone had ever played it before, the watch ticking out the time.

Picasso turned and left the café. As the door closed behind him with a slight bang, Django shuddered, but his clock eye, his licorice mustache, his table leg, all held fast. Django saw the spidery hands of time cast onto the café scene, saw faint numbers around the periphery of the room; and then he felt the back of the watch open, and the Plain of Rectangular Configuration appeared, and he was looking both ways at once. He saw Mignonne, and he went for her.

Argos made a grab for Django, but the Gypsy was like smoke from a Gauloise, swirling in Argos's hands. A moment later, and he was gone, leaving behind the semblance of himself Picasso had stuck together. The stick figure swayed on its chair leg, twisted its licorice mustache, and stared madly at Argos through its clock eye.

Django's two halves came together with a quiet sound, like dough being slapped. 'Ah! The rest of my ass!'

'Now can you get us out of this place?' demanded Mignonne.

'The lost chord has been found. Django is himself once more. He can do anything.' He began a closer examination of the wooden plain. It was endless marquetry, depicting moths, their wings delicate blond veneer; and crickets, shining in ebony; and cicadas of red cedar.

'Some poor woman probably has to polish all this,' said Mignonne.

'While we're here,' said Django, 'we must find Loli.'

'Why, have you got something going with her?'

'I'm sympathetic,' said the guitarist. 'It's my nature.'

'It's late, I'm tired, I should be in bed.'

Mignonne led the way, her heels clicking on the marquetry patterns, over images of snakes, dinosaurs, monkeys. Django followed behind her, looking left and right, then at Mignonne's tight skirt ahead of him, hips swiftly swinging back and forth. 'You're a determined chanteuse.' A chain smoker, and one known to drink strong perfume when the booze ran out, he was not in the best of shape, and walking had never come easy to him. Fishing, that's what he liked. He looked around for a pond, but a large inlaid oval mirror was all he found. 'This is the strangest place a Gypsy ever landed in.'

'Don't talk to me about Gypsies.'

Mignonne continued hurrying forward, Django coughing to keep up on the polished, slippery floor. 'When you're fresh, when you're rested, do you take whole blocks in your stride?'

Mignonne turned on him abruptly. 'A photographer was supposed to drop by tonight and do my portrait.'

'He'll have to drop clear out of the world to keep that appointment.'

Mignonne glared to Django, tiny electric fires in her pupils. 'One tries to make it in Paris, and it's hard enough. What if I'm missing a big break?'

'Look around you,' said Django, impatiently. 'The scenery moves with us as we walk. I nearly lost half my body. And you're worried about a break?'

'I don't accept interference in my life. That's how I got where I am.'

Django covered his eyes with the back of his hand. 'Talk to the stones, Django. They listen more closely than a Parisian nightingale.'

'Stop muttering.'

'I shall mutter without pause if I so desire.' He lowered his hand and gazed ahead. The rocks, like humpbacked reptiles, seemed to move just slightly, as if indicating a direction that might prove fruitful. He pointed, past the rocks, and Mignonne nodded. 'I'm a girl of the gutter, who followed an organ grinder around. Papa and I were here once, I think . . . '

Django was recalling a field somewhere north of Paris, where his family's caravan had stopped long ago, and their troupe of Gypsy comedians had entertained. Strange visitors had arrived, dancing to the Gypsy violins, and though he'd searched for that field many times after in years to come, he'd never found it again. Those dancing visitors, their bodies were like silk. 'Mignonne, I too may have been to this place before.'

'A gentleman took us back to his home to play for him,' said Mignonne. 'His living room had a sort of endless carpet.' She saw it now, the bygone living room suggesting itself, very discreetly, on all sides of her, as if she'd never escaped it. 'My father pretended nothing was wrong, we needed the money, but I looked at that gentleman and saw – he was a box.'

Django stood on tiptoe, trying to see over the horizon. 'Were we in a balloon, it would probably be less confusing.'

'A balloon? Is that all you can think of? Can't you be more resourceful?'

Django touched at his little mustache. 'The men of my line are not required to be resourceful. They must dress well, gamble, drink, and play music.'

'How convenient.'

'Occasionally we repair furniture.'

Mignonne pointed to the inlaid pattern ahead of them; set in woods of varying shades and sizes were their own likenesses, perfectly rendered. 'It's clad me in only my slip.'

'And I, beside you, naked as a baby.'

'Put some clothes on.'

'I'm not responsible for the dress code here. If the floor wishes to portray me in the altogether, that's its business.'

Mignonne bent forward, staring at the floor, and a blush came to her cheeks. 'Now my slip is gone too.'

The floor toyed with its own ideas of Django and Mignonne, keeping pace with them as they walked on,

51

its depictions of them increasing in intimacy.

'Don't look,' said Mignonne.

'I can't walk with my eyes closed.'

'Then turn your head sideways.'

'And get a crick in the neck?'

'You arranged this, didn't you?'

'I do not speak the language of hardwood floors.'

'Look – no don't – our figures are embracing! And now—!'

'The missionary position.'

'We're walking,' she commanded. 'Straight ahead with our eyes on the horizon.'

They walked on, Django stealing glances at the floor and humming a love song about a man covering his mistress with camelias as she lay in bed. The wooden mirror responded, entwining Mignonne's image with flowers. 'There,' said Django, 'we're hidden within them. Only the leaves move a little bit, just above your—'

'That's enough, I can see for myself.'

'It seems to be a simple creature,' said Django, 'and open to suggestion.'

And the floor became a design of many flowers, multiplying on vines and runners, growing in all directions, Django and Mignonne apparently forgotten.

Cocteau and Bombyx – wandering in the encampment of the Silks. Tents, and banners, and inhabitants who were themselves tents and banners. Firelight – and the scarves. Bombyx – the moth's dream. She was loose, draped over Cocteau's arm and neck, and her trailing edge was wrapped around his ankle. His exquisitely long fingers, the longest in Europe, played almost absentmindedly with her delicate form. She sighed, and slipped around his waist. 'I knew that I would fall in love with you tonight. Silk is electric and so easily excited.'

Cocteau himself was falling, into the past, his memory silk itself, a long unbroken thread unwinding now around the tiny worm hidden at its core. 'As a boy,' said Cocteau, 'I watched with envy my mother's crucial feminine gestures. To find again that gaslight where she dressed, in her gown of red, this I call beauty. I call it – Bombyx.'

'You know that my color isn't natural?' Bombyx indicated the splashes of golds and iridescent blues that covered her form. 'I've been bleached and dyed.'

'I have secrets too,' said Cocteau, discovering them only at this moment as Bombyx slipped her luminous folds across his brow, allowing him to follow the baffling logic of personality – his destiny had been shaped by the tiny jet beads sewn to his mother's opera gown, an arrangement that glistened like fish eggs, and from which his own erotic design had been hatched.

'There are velvets of gold,' said Bombyx, 'woven by the masters of Genoa. I'm just a simple handkerchief from Lyons.'

Cocteau's fingers continued to explore her fabric. 'Your sex is – indeterminate?'

'I accommodate.' Bombyx smiled, a crease created in her folds, but Cocteau's attention was gathered upon the essential moment in his mother's boudoir, with his life's struggle taking shape. 'Her fan was black lace, her hand a peacock, spreading itself; no one can resist such seduction. Was I male or female? Bombyx, you are my earliest dilemma. You are the thing I sought to become, male and female woven in one.'

The other veils, jealous perhaps, fluttered around Cocteau and Bombyx, and worked a bit of tawdry enchantment; Cocteau thought himself in Toulon, on the waterfront, with young sailors, bright scarves around their necks. He danced to 'Bolero de Django,' and Bombyx was left alone. 'The handkerchief is tossed aside,' she wept, her corners crumpling, 'He's not the first. I've been shoved in a drawer before.'

A blue-black sailor was Cocteau's partner, the sailor dancing with his kit bag slung over his shoulder.

'So, *may suhr*, we meet again.'

The two men danced – one through the secrets of his sponge, the other through his scarves, and where they truly were, which world was theirs, they could not say.

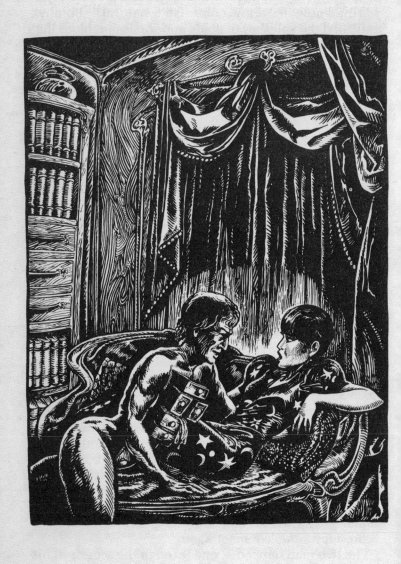

The blue man of Tierra del Fuego moved his lips closer to Cocteau's ear as they danced, and whispered a poem in the language of dolphins. Cocteau vanished from his arms, whispering 'one wakes alone,' and the blue man was jerked awake, upon the sands where he lay, his sponge beside him. 'So,' he said to himself, 'may suhr is gone.' And he smiled, and lay back upon the sands, his gaze traveling far out over the bright surface of the sea.

And Loli? The box had magicked her off to Box Land where, in a more congenial and fluid dimension, he had the shape of a man. He was, of course, still a box, a fact that could not be disguised, for he had drawers coming out of his anatomy in various and, one might say, strategic places. Loli took in few of these details, for she was angry.

'You've abducted me, monsieur.'

'My ways are crude, for I'm only a box. But night after night your hair caressed my hinges. Was I to go mad?'

'It's no concern of mine.' Loli allowed herself to gaze around the box's chambers. They were tastefully furnished, the colors subdued, the lighting muted, and a thick Arabian carpet imparted a solemn hush to the atmosphere. A six-legged desk, a Chinese screen embroidered with silk, chairs covered in viridian velvet, a collection of classics bound in scarlet morocco – these were a few of the things Loli saw as she tried to estimate what sort of hands she'd fallen into. The dark accents were soothing. Or was it all an elaborate trap meant to disarm a young woman? Rich oak paneling covered the walls, and curtains trimmed with tassels and old braid gave the windows a dignified glow, yet there was something studied about the arrangement, something that put Loli off. The box paced nervously. 'Nightly my doors closed upon you. Nightly you squeezed yourself out through my false back panel. Am I made of stone? I am wood, and fine-grained.'

'We're supposed to be professionals.' Loli moved away from a glowing table lamp, conscious that it shone through the flimsy material of her costume.

The box did not try to close the distance between them. 'I wished only to know you better. Can you forgive me?'

'Absolutely not.'

'This has never happened before. I have had a long career.'

'Too long, I think.'

The box bowed. 'I was made by Bartl and Willmann Combined Magical Apparatus of Hamburg, a firm of the highest ethical standards.'

'Well, somebody taught you very bad manners.'

'I've worked in low places, of course.' The box switched on music, the persuasive guitar of Django Reinhardt sounding softly in the background.

Loli forced him to meet her gaze. 'I trusted you. You were like a grandfather clock.'

'I've a cousin who's a clock.' The box smiled, a faint trace of superiority on his lips. 'A steady pendulum in his loins, mechanical birds in his head to sing the hour. It is a charming life. He is a scholar of time. But – he has never loved.'

'A girl would feel safe with him,' said Loli.

'But how long would his monotonous ticking satisfy her?'

'You know nothing of women.'

'I have worked with dozens of magician's assistants,' said the box proudly.

'And did you abduct them all?'

He opened a drawer in his chest, reached into it. 'Please, have a mint.'

'No, thank you. I can't accept sweets from my abductor.'

'Won't you think of me as a suitor?' He opened a drawer in his forehead and handed her a tiny leather-bound volume. 'I am studying *The Human Comedy*, by your Monsieur Balzac. Soon I shall know enough to be human myself.'

'It will take more than a book,' said Loli, tossing it into an armchair.

The box took her hand tenderly in his. 'The warm

touch of your fingers on my drawers, that is what I need.'

'A very coarse suggestion.'

'Is it? I didn't know, I am screwed together. You must instruct me – how should I woo you?'

'I'm not about to instruct you.' Loli removed her hand from his. 'And I could never feel affection for someone who holds me against my will.'

'Oh, I don't know. You might grow used to me after a while.'

Loli moved away dramatically, as LeBlanc had trained her to do on stage, her head tilted at an angle, the back of her wrist lightly touching her cheek. 'I shall languish here. A young girl can't be kept in a box. I need sunlight and wine.'

'Don't you know sunlight fades one's veneer? As for wine—' The box opened another drawer in his chest and brought out a bottle and two glasses. Loli let her gaze return to him. His cologne had a trace of aromatic cedar in it, a suggestion of the hallowed and old, of something precious stored away for years; there was a comfortable avuncularity about him, faintly familiar, that of a naughty uncle from her childhood. In spite of herself, she softened, just a little.

The half of Django that Picasso had constructed out of odds and ends hopped out of the café, and though Argos and the American expatriate saxophonist went chasing after it, the thing was too clever for them, and too fast; it teetered off on its own down a dark street, and vanished, only to cause a stir later at a lowlife dance hall near the boulevard de Sébastopol, where it was knocked apart by a hotheaded mobster who caught it dancing with his girl. The broken pieces were tossed out back, and no one said any more about it.

Argos and the American expatriate saxophonist found themselves walking along the Seine embankment, accompanied by Babette and Giselle. The American expatriate saxophonist was indulging in some gloom.

'Everybody who was, is dead, Argos, have you ever thought of that? Napoleon rode through these streets, believing his own hot jazz was here to stay.'

'We lost some people,' said Argos, 'We'll get them back. No need to grow melancholy.'

'Yes, cheer up,' said Babette, 'you've got us.'

'We're all just bones,' said the American expatriate saxophonist. 'A hedge in the park lives longer.'

'He is down in the dumps, isn't he,' said Giselle.

'He's an American expatriate saxophonist,' explained Argos.

'The great Django Reinhardt, gone, just like that.' The American expatriate saxophonist snapped his American expatriate finges, and cast a mournful gaze toward the dark Seine flowing past.

'Has he ever disappeared before?' asked Babette, for whom disappearing men were the rule.

'Sure,' said Argos, 'he forgets recording dates, he doesn't show up at the club, and then we find him playing banjos with the Gypsies in a camp north of Paris.'

'But,' said the American expatriate saxophonist, 'he never disappeared in the smoke from a Gauloise before.'

'I didn't want to say anything,' said Giselle, 'but I wouldn't have trusted my missing side to Picasso. He might give you a doorknob for your left titty.'

Babette tightened the short white scarf she wore at her neck, believing it protected her from the dampness encountered on the steps of the hotels of Les Halles. 'I could have gotten the rest of Django back. You pull slowly and speak softly, and little by little you reel him in. I once had nothing left of a stevedore but his nose.'

The little group walked along a street of antique shops, the two women dawdling at a display of heirloom brooches, hatpins, rings. 'I'm hearing Django's music again,' said Babette.

'I always hear it,' said Argos. 'The "Limehouse Blues." '

'It seems to be coming from this shop window.' Babette peered toward a corner of the window lit by the faint glow of a streetlamp. 'That table over there is playing a tune.'

'The top of it is inlaid,' said Babette, pressing her nose against the glass. 'With the figures of a man and a woman.'

'Look what they're doing,' said Giselle, 'that's some hot jazz for you.'

'That's Django and Mignonne!' cried Argos.

'She really has him entwined,' said Babette.

'Give them some privacy,' said the American expatriate saxophonist.

'If they're going to do it on top of a table in a shop window, darling, I'd say privacy isn't uppermost in their minds. I mean, they could have used a tablecloth.'

'We must buy that table. '

'One, you have no money. Two, the shop is closed.'

'Well then—'

Argos looked up and down the street, then put his elbow through the glass. The two musicians grabbed the table and ran with it, Babette and Giselle close behind.

In the somber chambers of the Vanishing Box, a pathetic scene was playing out, the box having gone down on his knees to Loli, knocking aside a Victorian footstool, crawling before her on his fine Oriental carpet. 'Please, let me just kiss your toes.'

'Not under any circumstances.' Loli pushed the footstool back between them. He hurled it aside in anguish.

'Have pity on me, for god's sake.'

'If you had courted me properly—'

'How? I am a *box!*'

Loli turned her back to him, pretending to study a lithograph on the wall. 'Love would have found a way.'

'But I do love you. I adore you. From the first moment you stepped inside me I've been hopelessly enslaved. Do you remember? You fumbled innocently with my secret latch, it slid open in your fingers, surprising you, shocking you perhaps, but shocking me still more deeply, for I'd never been opened quite that way before, with such a childlike caress.' The box, regaining some

60

measure of dignity, scrambled to his feet again. 'Certainly there were others before you, I'll not deny it, but they were hardened chorus girls, they went in and out of me as if I were a broom closet.'

'What an old lecher.'

'Say rather, my wood is seasoned.'

'And you're much too slick.'

'Just my veneer.'

Loli put him at arm's length again, moving beneath a pair of carved gilded wall sconces. As if a connoisseur of such things, she caressed their golden leaves. 'You should meet another box.'

He pretended to center a painted stoneware jar in its place atop a bookshelf. 'It's true I've had affairs. A lovely little jewel box and I—' He turned toward Loli. 'She was plush black velvet inside, and had a mirror attached to her lid, that *was* exciting—'

'I don't wish to hear.'

'No, certainly not. In any case, how could she compare with you, Loli? You, my dear, know how to make a box feel young again. Look, look how my hinges glow!' He twisted his elbows and wrists.

Loli moved down the length of the room, letting one arm trail melodramatically behind her; she was only a magician's assistant, after all. He followed her, and she moved behind a loveseat upholstered in dark velvet, her fingers drawing lines in the fabric as she gazed at him. 'What am I to do with you, I wonder?'

'One kiss, Loli, one only. This much for the box you work with, to keep him going night after night.' He knelt on the loveseat before her. He attempted to look cuddlesome, harmless. His hand closed over hers, gently. She found herself staring at his fingernails, her face reflected in miniature in their gleaming brass; the intriguing aroma of his cedarwood cologne reached her again. When he raised himself toward her, she allowed his lips to meet hers.

His kiss tasted sweet, the faintest trace of running sap on his tongue. He brought her down beside him on the loveseat; in his excitement he allowed one of his drawers to fall open. Loli glanced into it, then reached in and pulled out a pair of silk stockings. 'And who do *these* belong to?'

'I – don't know. Someone must have – must have stuffed them in there.'

'And this?' She held up a lace garter belt.

'How odd, the things one finds . . . '

'You have someone living here.'

'She was just passing through me . . . darling girl . . . please . . .' The box regained the advantage, his lips brushing Loli's again, even as she tried to turn her head away. The taste of his mouth, with its pure, thin sweetness, was irresistible. Her lips opened, the box whispering, 'Put your hand on my drawer . . . there . . . yes . . . now open it . . . close it . . . faster . . . yes . . . oh yes . . . '

The box sighed, and Loli felt a secret little compartment open in her as well, and a hand with rootlike fingers reached into it and removed a small scented pillow. '*This is what you feel,*' said a soft voice, and it was what she felt, now that it was pointed out, a feeling so fleeting she might have missed it altogether, indeed had missed it many times in life before, a tiny bit of comfort from the dark interior. The love of a box, she said to herself, is not altogether to be despised. She felt him shudder, heard him gasp, and opening her eyes, saw he'd collapsed into unconsciousness, his body slipping off the loveseat and falling onto the floor, obviously not used to the excitement of human warmth, in spite of his previous affairs.

A door to the chamber opened, and a veil entered. 'Quick . . . while he's still unhinged.'

'Too late,' said Loli, 'we're lovers now.'

'You run a terrible risk.'

'I think he cherishes me. No man has done as much.'

'I beg you, reconsider.'

'And who are you?'

'I am Bombyx. Man of silk.'

* * *

62

LeBlanc gestured toward the scenery that was following him. 'It makes me nervous, Woo. One can't seem to adjust to it.'

Sing Woo brought out a cigarette, tore it to shreds, rolled the bits in his hands, and then produced it whole again, with a flick of his wrist. He lit it and blew smoke at LeBlanc. 'Your little tart of an assistant – describe her for me.'

'Just over five feet, small bones. Perfect for a box trick. Why do you ask? Do you get such a variety of assistants floating around over here?'

'Only curious, LeBlanc. One never knows. I should not like to send you back with the wrong assistant.' Sing Woo inhaled on his cigarette. A second later he exhaled the smoke through the hole in his chest.

LeBlanc gazed at it appreciatively. 'A nice trick. It's done with a hose of some sort?'

'It's done with a bullet hole in the chest.'

'Ah yes, I'd forgotten.' LeBlanc looked suspiciously at Woo's exhalations, to see where the sleight of hand was hidden. 'Don't suppose you'd want to share it with me.'

'I give it to you without charge, LeBlanc: When we find your assistant, or any assistant, have her fire a Sturm Ruger Blackhawk revolver at point blank range into your chest. All else will follow upon that.'

Ahead of them was a pot of fire, burning on a tripod. To the right of it was a feeding dove, pecking at the wooden floor. The sense of an abandoned act was in it, the dreary emptiness of a trick that has died. 'These altars,' said Sing Woo, 'are placed throughout the land, in memory of faded conjurors. The dove remains near this station, always, waiting for her master.'

'And who might that be?'

'It could be anyone. It could be you, LeBlanc.'

Have I faded? LeBlanc asked himself. *Does the lonely dove wait for me?*

'This land can get you down,' said Sing Woo. 'Unless you keep your touch.' A rose of coins appeared in his hands, neatly framed in his fingers. A moment more, and the coins had vanished again. 'All we are is a trick or two, eh, LeBlanc? Our life a little piece of the illusionist's art?'

'I could do without the Chinese double-talk, Woo, if you don't mind.' LeBlanc was disturbed. The plain of wooden flooring, the scenery that was following him like an animal – it made him uneasy. 'What do you do for an audience in these parts?' he asked, turning back toward Sing Woo.

'Big problem. You can play to the silk crowd, but they never get the point of the trick. I mean, they're just a bunch of stupid handkerchiefs.'

'This lack of an audience increases my determination to find Loli at once, Woo, and get out of here. I hope we're getting closer?'

'See those banners on the horizon? That's where the boxes are.'

'Boxes?'

'Magic cabinets, LeBlanc. This is where they come from.'

'Mine came from Hamburg, old chap.'

'Yes, but this is where the thought of it was conceived. It's called the Plain of Rectangular Conjuration.'

'Lot of boxes?'

'Exactly.'

'I don't trust it.'

'No, of course not.' Sing Woo's eyes narrowed, as he gazed toward the horizon. 'Boxes can be dangerous.'

'And sly. Nothing so sly as a box, Woo. I know that now.'

Sing Woo and LeBlanc approached the plain of the boxes cautiously. The great box doors of the city gate swung open for them, and they entered. The streets were crowded with boxes of every variety, and LeBlanc and Sing Woo threaded their way through. 'Are they aware of us?' asked LeBlanc.

'Hard to say. Right now they seem to just be clunking and bumping around like the dull brutes they are. But one never knows.' Sing Woo squeezed between two of them, and LeBlanc followed quickly, with no desire to

64

be crushed by a pair of packing crates. He hurried on after Sing Woo, but a small chest intervened, opening its lid to LeBlanc, and emitting an aroma so familiar that LeBlanc staggered toward it drunkenly. 'The toy chest – of my childhood—'

A hand gripped him roughly, yanking him back. 'Careful LeBlanc, they are like flytraps, you know.'

'Ah, but this chest contains the secrets of my earliest inspiration.'

'It read your memory, they're good at that.' Sing Woo had to struggle to move LeBlanc along the street. 'It would have slowly digested you.'

'Woo, I've been transported. I practiced my first tricks with a chest like that.'

'Conjuration, LeBlanc, don't be a mark.'

LeBlanc staggered on, only slowly regaining his self-control. By the time he'd straightened his cuffs he was himself again. 'I'm grateful to you, Woo. I almost went under.'

'The dream inside a box is a long one.' Sing Woo continued weaving through the crowd, then pointed to a high prominence above the town – a hill on which a massive gleaming Chinese cabinet stood. 'That's the top drawer. We've got to talk to it. Have you got an offering?'

'LeBlanc offers magic nightly.'

The two magicians climbed the hill, up a flight of winding wooden steps, each of which was a drawer. One of them opened, causing LeBlanc to step in it. 'Sorry, so sorry—' But looking down he saw twisted nail tricks, comic eggs, colored balls, enchanted rings, bent keys – all items from his earliest boyhood routines. 'Woo, look what's here, this stuff is precious, this—'

'The drawer is magicking you, LeBlanc, come on.'

'Yes, yes, but—' LeBlanc stumbled upward, dragged by Woo. 'How is it you're not affected, Woo?'

'Once you've had daylight shot through you, LeBlanc, it's very simple.'

Woo led them to the top of the stairs and bowed before

the great emperor cabinet. Its black lacquer finish was dazzling, and, in the milky depths of its mother-of-pearl inlay, scenes of the ancient court life moved, with human courtiers depicted in their pleadings for position, information, escape from the Plain of Rectangular Conjuration; their pale faces swam up to the surface, mouths silently working. LeBlanc stared at it in wonder. A box like this could be an asset to an act. If I made an offer?

'Your Majesty,' said Sing Woo, 'we lower our heads.'

Could it refuse? If I mentioned the clubs I'll be playing at next winter on the Riviera? What the devil is Woo muttering?

'Majesty, we offer for your pleasure a sample of our latest, most up-to-date routines. Beside me is LeBlanc, master of coins, flowers, silks, and the fast deck.'

LeBlanc stepped forward. 'Happy to demonstrate, Your Majesty, but before I do, I'd like to make you a small proposition concerning a tour I'll be making – a first-class tour, let me hasten to add, and one on which I shall provide every comfort within reason. Your share of the revenue will be settled upon at a later date, but I assure you—'

An elbow caught LeBlanc in the ribs, and Sing Woo hissed in his ear, *'This is royalty, you fool! Do you want to get us beheaded?'*

'Nothing up my sleeve, Majesty, observe my cuffs.'

Cocteau walked among the Silks, their ends curling around his ankles and wrists as he passed, but he'd remembered why he'd come and ignored their seductions. 'Where is Loli?' he demanded of the Chief of Silks.

'Bombyx has her,' said the Chief, who was a large rolled scarf adorned with gold napkin rings. 'But why do you wish to return to that heaviness of flesh?'

'My thoughts here, while perfectly beautiful, stream away before I can arrange them.'

'I never keep my guests by force,' said the Chief.

Cocteau threaded his way between the gaudy tents of the silks, until he came to the edge of the encampment.

No one tried to prevent his leaving. Once more he was on the parquet plain, where he was awaited by a sculpted figure of ebony whose outline, even before he was near, revealed it to be that of a fellow Frenchman. The statue, as Cocteau came closer, bowed. 'Allow me to introduce myself. I am the mysterious figure Alfreyd O. Montagne Ené de Piro.'

'Permit me to observe,' said Cocteau, 'that you are also a statue.'

'More importantly, I am an anagram that shall remain unsolved.' It walked beside Cocteau with silent step. 'I might possibly be of assistance, though perhaps you wish no intrusions?'

Before Cocteau could answer, the statue raised its arm, pointing. Django Reinhardt and Mignonne were approaching.

'Cocteau!' Django hurried forward, dragging Mignonne. 'What a relief to see you. Have you discovered anything?'

'Loli has changed hands. The box no longer has her.' He turned to the chanteuse. 'I hope you are not too distressed, Mademoiselle Mignonne.'

'I'm not at my best, Monsieur Cocteau. My voice feels thin.'

'What's this statue, Cocteau? The eyes open and shut.' Django circled round the sculpture, examining it closely. He tapped on its polished forehead.

'I am Alfreyd O. Montagne Ené de Piro, at your service,' said the statue.

'I don't know what your connection is to this place,' said Django, 'but I hesitate to tell you what your floor has been up to.'

'I've been studying the scheme of things,' said Cocteau. 'Everything is faintly familiar and holds a tiny tantalizing center, but all meaning collapses when we draw near.'

'And where is Loli?' asked Django.

Before Cocteau could answer, the statue of Alfreyd O. Montagne Ené de Piro pointed toward the horizon, which was rising up with a creaking groan, in one long flat surface. 'It is hinged,' said the statue.

On all four sides, then, the horizon of wood rose up, and when the sides were erected a lid came down, and Cocteau, Django Reinhardt, Mignonne, and the statue were imprisoned in the darkness of a large box.

'What do we do?' Cocteau asked the statue.

'We take our time.'

Easy for you,' said Cocteau. He lit a match and gazed at the statue's dark face. 'Who made you?'

'The shadows made Alfreyd O. Montagne Ené de Piro.'

As for Django, when the lid came down, he put his arm around Mignonne. 'Do you hear?' A recording of the Hot Jazz Trio playing 'Blue Light Blues' was coming from the walls somewhere, and Django brought Mignonne against him and began to dance, but she pushed him away. 'How many wives have you had?'

'You ask me that at a time like this?'

'How many?'

'Two only. The first one made artificial flowers.' Django tried to slip his hand back around Mignonne's waist. 'And you? Any ties?'

'That's none of your business.'

'I bare my soul to you, and I get nothing in return?'

'Telling me your first wife made artificial flowers is not baring your soul.'

'My second wife had rosy cheeks. There.'

'There what?'

'Now you know it all.' Django gave her his winsome smile, the one he felt brought out maternal feelings in women.

Mignonne looked away in disgust. 'If I had to disappear, why couldn't it have been with an adventurer of some kind, a soldier perhaps, or someone useful, like a mechanic.'

'I have my good angles.'

'A real man would be building a shelter, sending up smoke signals, finding us food . . . '

Django's music came in softly again, and his hand slipped back around her waist. 'My little parakeet, my angel, my canary . . . '

'You damned Gypsy . . . ' His smooth-soled shoes moved between her high heels. A small spot fell upon them, shining down from high up in the lid of the box, onto Mignonne's dark hair and bare shoulders, and smoke curled in the beam as they danced through it. The spotlight changed from white to blue, and they moved like a pair of cranes. A brass bed rolled up to them; upon the bed hung a bow; music was scattered on the sheets. 'Why,' said Django, 'this is Argos's bed.'

'How did it get here?'

'The night provides.'

Mignonne stared down at it. 'I'm going to be run through by another jazz musician.'

'I'll take you fishing,' said Django. 'We'll pack a picnic basket, then buy a Rolls-Royce and get a chauffeur to drive us in it as fast as it will go.'

'But when I'm old,' said Mignonne, thoughtfully, 'and hear your music on some rusty Victrola . . . '

'You'll think, *that was Django.*'

'Your Majesty, that ends my magic sampling for this afternoon.' LeBlanc bowed. 'The complete show will be performed in the evening, at your convenience, for a nominal fee. My secretary, Mr. Woo, will handle the details.'

'*I'm not your bloody secretary.*'

'Mr. Woo asks me to remind you that your entire court is invited to attend. The fee is slightly higher, but the effects with a larger audience are in some ways more startling.' LeBlanc withdrew, and Sing Woo stepped up to the Royal Cabinet.

'Excellency, if you have enjoyed our performance, we beg that you bestow a boon on us. We have lost our assistant, a young woman named Loli, rumored to be somewhere in your great city.'

A small door in the side of the cabinet opened. Sing Woo and LeBlanc peered in, and heard the sound of a music box. Then a ghostly shape, of Loli in miniature, wandered across a tiny red-curtained stage. A backdrop

descended, revealing the walls of a shabby hotel, and Loli was walking its hall, in the company of Bombyx.

'That's she,' said LeBlanc. 'But who's that she's with?'

'One of the handkerchief crowd. Very smooth with the ladies.'

'Her contract expressly states – no romantic involvement. I can't have trained assistants falling in love, it ruins their timing.'

'I recognize the place. It's a fleabag hotel, not far from here.'

The imperial boon having been bestowed, the door of the emperor cabinet closed upon the miniature tableau. LeBlanc turned to Sing Woo. 'The automatisms of this box are remarkable. I haven't seen anything like that since Robert-Houdin's mechanical butterflies.'

Sing Woo bowed to the Royal Cabinet. 'Your Majesty, we are ever in your debt. You are a gracious sovereign.'

LeBlanc and Sing Woo descended the royal staircase. 'That cabinet was one in a million, Woo. The man who made it was a craftsman of the first rank.'

'It was not made by human hands.'

'You're not playing to the rubes now, this is LeBlanc. I mean to have that thing.'

LeBlanc outlined a scheme, which Sing Woo ignored. They reached the city street. 'The hotel we seek,' said Sing Woo, 'is that way, if I remember correctly.' He pointed up the block.

'You know your way around, Woo. You lack imagination, but you clearly understand the territory. I'm beginning to see – this place could be included on my tour. There aren't any people around just now, but my four-color poster will bring them out. It's a marvelous thing, made by Artistic Lithographs of London, Limited.'

'I hope your assistant is quick-witted, LeBlanc.'

'I like this town, Woo. Something about it – a sort of grand solemnity. One thinks big here, about the big illusions. One can make an elephant and two camels disappear – if the box is large enough. And they've got them, Woo. Look around you.'

They entered the hallway of the cheap hotel. Sing Woo peered up the stairs. 'She's gone, LeBlanc. Look.' Upon the paneled wall of the staircase the shadow of a woman remained, walking slowly but absorbed into wood that appeared to be using her for its own pleasure, the panels oozing a strong smell of lemon-scented polish from deep in the grain. Loli's shadow descended the oaken stairs and glided along the floor, but at the doorway could go no farther. The shadow turned, seeming to face LeBlanc and Sing Woo. *Gentlemen, I am being violated in the most foul way.*

'Let's get out of here, LeBlanc, these walls are filthy with tricks. It will grab our shadows too.'

'LeBlanc's shadow has something to say about that.' LeBlanc raised his hand before the bare bulb of the hall so that it cast the heads of animals in silhouette on the wall. Loli's shadow turned, fascinated by a creature that was now a deer, now a giraffe, now a pachyderm with swinging trunk. Loli's shadow followed LeBlanc's menagerie along the wall, and the wall's grip on her loosened as LeBlanc led the feminine thing out through the door, to the street, where it flew quickly away.

'Nice work, LeBlanc! Now,' cried Sing Woo, 'we must follow it!'

They followed, not knowing they'd just been fast-carded by a handkerchief; the shadow of Loli was a piece of deception spun by Bombyx to throw off pursuers. He and Loli were upstairs in the hotel, Loli in his embrace, his folds caressing her ankles, her wrists. She turned away from him, toward the shabby wallpaper of the room. 'First a box, now a handkerchief. I'm sleeping around too casually. And I hardly know you.'

'I am Bombyx Mori, of the distinguished family Bombycidae of North China and Bengal. You could have run into others, made from waste silk. Trashy fellows, at best. My family has been used in the making of ecclesiastical vestments for centuries.'

'You didn't seem ecclesiastical about five minutes ago.' Loli's gaze wandered from the wall to the ceiling, where a bare bulb hung lopsidedly on a twisted cord. 'And why do I feel so sad?'

'Because of me,' said Bombyx. 'The pupas are killed, you see. They can't be allowed to live, for if they emerged as moths from their cocoons the precious thread would be torn many times, and the Empress of China can't have that. So I carry in me that little death, that dream of flight that never was, in order that the thread be unbroken, two thousand feet long.'

Bombyx's voice was a peculiar whispering, the sensation that of breath passing lightly through Loli's nerves. 'The Chinese guarded the true knowledge of the cocoon for a thousand years. The penalty for revealing it was death. And then – two Nestorian monks smuggled some moth eggs in a hollow staff to Constantinople. Never trust a tie salesman or a priest, as the saying goes.'

Loud noises came to them through the walls, for a party was going on next door, boxes thumping and creaking, their hinges groaning wildly. One of them was a music box, and its tune would pop out each time its lid was knocked open. 'That song could drive one mad,' said Loli.

'A cheap box, from the sound of it.'

'What sort of party are they having?'

'They're rather crude, as I think you've discovered.'

Loli listened to the boxes rolling around drunkenly, crashing into each other, their overturned castors spinning. 'My abductor was – considerate – in his own way. I felt sorry for him.'

'Eventually he would have smothered you. Not intentionally, of course. But boxes can be appallingly stupid.'

'And you creatures of silk?'

His smooth fabric slipped between her thighs. 'Silk is made for intimacy.'

'And what am I made for, I wonder? To be shut up in a box, nightly?' She slid off the bed, took her magician's assistant's costume from the edge of a chair. The fabric seemed rough and cheap; living silk had spoiled her. 'I feel something inside me drifting, as if I were coming apart, very slowly.'

73

Bombyx crossed to her at the foot of the bed. 'I spin as the silkworm spins, round and round you, spinnerets at my lips, my kisses green silk flowers—'

'On stage I wear a lot of makeup. Men think I'm a tart. You'll still love me when I'm old?'

'I myself will be faded and torn,' said Bombyx, and his lithe form folded in upon itself, over and over, until he was a small square of silk in the middle of the bed. Loli put him in her blouse, against her breast. He was just a handkerchief and she only a magician's assistant, but silk can make one feel good about oneself; with Bombyx counseling her heart, she opened the door and stepped outside into the hall of the hotel as if she were a headliner. A box from the party next door crashed into the hall at the same time; perceiving her confident bearing, it restrained itself and tipped its lid in a gentlemanly fashion. 'That's better,' said Loli, and brushed on past it, not noticing that the wall of the hotel was sucking her shadow into the grain. She heard a faint tearing sound, but at the same moment the drunken box grew ill, heaved drunkenly open, and spilled out the contents of a long night's debauchery onto the hall floor. 'Poor thing,' said Loli to herself, and walked on, minus her own darkness.

It's mine, chuckled the wall to itself, savoring the flavor of all of Loli's little secrets, as walls will.

Cocteau walked through the dimly lit world of the box, calling for Django. A forest intervened and he had no choice but to enter it. Upon closer examination he discovered that the tree trunks were actually closed umbrellas. Each of them bore the tag of a Paris store, and upon one of them he found the bill, made out to an M. Satie. 'The hundred umbrellas of Erik Satie!' cried Cocteau. He moved from umbrella to umbrella. Some of them were still wrapped in shop paper. 'He never uses them. Just buys them, likes to have them, and here they are.'

A clap of thunder struck the air, and the boxed-in

sky lifted open, as did the hundred umbrellas of Satie, which raised themselves over Cocteau and soon were reverberating with the sound of raindrops. Gentle piano music accompanied the rain, and Cocteau perceived a small rotund figure approaching, his face like two half-moons, his carriage that of a minor civil servant.

'Satie!' cried Cocteau. 'Are you a prisoner in this land too!'

'I?' replied Satie. 'A prisoner? I should say not. Have your movements been restricted in some way, Cocteau?'

'No, but—'

'Then what are you complaining about? You're too sensitive. Bathing with water is your problem. I use a pumice stone myself. It toughens the hide.' Satie scratched his goatee between every two words.

Cocteau peered out from beneath the pattering umbrellas, across the vast wooden plain. 'How do you come and go from this place?'

'My dear fellow, I write my scores in red ink without bar lines. You surely can find your own way out of here.'

Cocteau peered through the curtain of rain. There, just beyond it was rue Grégoire-de-Tours. He lurched toward the street, but it rotated away from him, leaving him standing in the rain on the Plain of the Rectangular Conjuration. He stepped back under the umbrellas. 'I missed the exit.'

'Musical lemonade, that's what we have these days, Cocteau. That is what I'm struggling against. Musical lollipops. And you talk of exits. I took the train from Monte Carlo to Paris and spent the night standing up in the corridor of the sleeping car. That is discipline.'

Cocteau wiped the rain from his forehead and, as he did so, remembered Loli. 'I'm here to rescue someone.'

'And I to rescue no one,' replied Satie. 'I am instead working on a new composition, which I call *Limp Preludes to a Dog*.'

'You seem comfortable here.'

'I'll tell you my secret, Cocteau. It is a precious one

and has saved me from a great deal of difficulty. I never open letters from friends. I do, however, send postcards to others. I am sending one to the music critic Poueigh, who has said I lack inventiveness, wit, and professional skill. Allow me to read you my reply: ' "Sir and dear friend, you're no more than an asshole – asshole without music".'

'I wouldn't send that if I were you, Satie.'

'It strikes exactly the right tone.'

'I have the certainty you will spend a week in jail for it.'

'Nonsense. And now, I shall play you *Pieces in the Shape of Pear*.'

Cocteau noticed a lemon dangling from the handle of an umbrella. 'Ah! I'm remembering a dream.'

'Please don't tell it to me.'

'I dreamt it while staying at the Hotel de Russia in the Piazza del Popolo in Rome.'

'Dreams are like letters,' grumbled Satie, 'better left unopened.'

Cocteau reached up to the hanging lemon and turned it slowly in his fingertips. 'I dreamt I'd stolen a lemon from the Pope's garden, and he chased me down the hallways of the Vatican.'

'Don't pick this one,' said Satie, 'or there'll be trouble.'

Cocteau picked the lemon.

'I warned you.'

Through the forest of umbrellas came a disconcerted Pope, holding up the hem of his white cassock as he ran toward Cocteau. 'Stop! Stop, thief!'

Cocteau fled, out of the forest. The Plain of Rectangular Conjuration went to work, erecting a long echoing hallway around him. Candelabra burned on either side, illuminating holy masterpieces framed in gold. He saw a door, opened it, and raced inside. Seated on a golden papal bed was Django, putting on his pants. Mignonne lay beside him in her slip.

'Cocteau!' cried Django. 'What's going on?'

The door burst open again, and the Pope confronted Cocteau.

'My lemon, please, monsieur.'

Cocteau, Django, and Mignonne backed across the room. *'Give him his infernal lemon, Cocteau,'* hissed Django.

But Cocteau refused to open his hand. 'Why am I compelled to pick it? The key to my whole life may be in this act.'

'Oh, for god's sake,' said Mignonne and, popping the lemon from Cocteau's hand, gave it to the Pope. 'There, Papa. Forgive us our sins.'

'Thank you, mademoiselle,' said the Pope, and withdrew. As the door closed behind him, the room, the papal hallway, and the bed vanished, and the Plain of Rectangular Conjuration appeared once more, with its flat unending floor. Cocteau, Django, and Mignonne were standing in the rain. 'So ends my dream each time,' sighed Cocteau.

'This place is getting on my nerves,' said Mignonne.

Cocteau moved slowly forward. 'In dreams, one can go through walls by pushing, if one believes. But here the walls come and go at will, too cunning to allow such elementary dreamer's tricks. Escape must come by other means.'

'Wandering is my style,' said Django. 'Hotels are what get me down. I've checked out with just my hat, many times.'

The rain turned to a fine mist that laid a net of tiny crystals in their hair. A pale sun, more like a huge, dim bulb, shone through the mist, finally scattering it, and Mignonne pointed toward the horizon. 'There's something ahead.' The wall of the city of boxes awaited them – dark, polished wood, somber in the sulphurous sunlight of the alien world.

They approached cautiously, but no one threatened them. The city walls swung open on great metal hinges. They entered the maze of boxed-in streets, down which other boxes thumped and rolled.

'How sweet,' said Mignonne, as a small white jewel box came by, like a dog, skittering between her feet.

Across the street, swiveling on castors in Cocteau's direction, was a familiar cabinet, its clear glass doors revealing a collection of Antinoüs masks, set on red velvet, their enameled eyes calling Cocteau into the land of their thoughts. 'Grandpapa!' he cried, and raced across the street toward his grandfather's cabinet.

'Come, little Jean,' said the cabinet. 'I will teach you the secret of the Masks.'

'Careful Cocteau,' said Django. 'A box took half my ass away.'

'Yes,' said Mignonne, 'and these jewels are fake.'

'Little Jean, my pet,' said the Grandfather cabinet, 'I'll let you smoke a Nazir cigarette in a bone holder. I have a silver bathtub you can ring like a gong.'

My earliest desires, thought Cocteau. He looked at Django. 'I'm being pulled back to my beginnings.'

'You'll find sitting down there a painful business, old man. I'm all for nostalgia but not at the price of losing half one's backside.'

The Grandfather cabinet opened its glass doors invitingly. 'Child, you may play with my Greek busts, my Florentine medals, my teardrop bottles . . . '

'There'll be tears all right,' said Django to Cocteau, 'when you're propped up by one cheek on a bar stool.'

'Come along, Monsieur Cocteau,' said Mignonne, 'I see nothing in that cabinet but shelf paper and shadows.'

'We'd better find a café,' said Django, and led his friends down the street, past squat, boxlike buildings, and into the first open doorway that he found. It was a sort of music hall they entered, with boxes lined up in the audience, thumping their doors in applause for a thing so tiny, so ridiculous but to them so funny – a mechanical mouse that rolled around the stage under the brilliant glare of a spotlight. It was followed by a pillar of dinner plates wobbling and swaying drunkenly across the stage, to the delight of the boxes, which emitted creaking noises, something like laughter but caused by the partial rapid opening and closing of their drawers.

Then, onto the stage stepped LeBlanc. 'Ladies and

78

gentlemen, welcome. I, LeBlanc, world-famous magician, am here to entertain you with tricks not seen since the time of Pharaoh, if that means anything to you, and perhaps it does, for the Egyptians invented the coffin. Now, my assistant, Hop Sing Woo, will bring on the goldfish.'

'What's he doing here?' hissed Django.

'And where is Loli?' asked Cocteau.

Mignonne went charging up the aisle toward the stage. 'LeBlanc, come down here, we're leaving! I have a photographic engagement in one hour!'

'Will the management please constrain the young woman? This is a professional show of international magic.'

But Mignonne had crawled up onto the stage. 'You faker! Where's Loli?'

'We were on her trail,' said Hop Sing Woo, 'but LeBlanc insisted we do a second matinee.'

'And who are you?'

'One who failed at the bullet-catching trick, mademoiselle. I had better luck producing doves and children from beneath a cloth, and should have stuck to it.'

'Well, produce Loli, so we can go. I'm sure she's as sick of this place as I.'

'On the contrary,' said Woo, 'it is our understanding she has fallen in love with a handkerchief.'

'How like her,' said Mignonne. 'While some of us have their career hanging in the balance.'

'As for careers,' said Sing Woo, 'I can only give this advice – do not try to catch live bullets with a plate, even when dressed as a Chinese warlord.'

'We're all grateful for your philosophical nuggets, Woo,' said LeBlanc, 'but may I remind you I'm waiting for the goldfish?'

The audience had been angered by the interruption and rose to its feet, doors slamming violently open and closed, and now some of the larger and more rowdy boxes were thumping down the aisle toward the stage.

'Honored guests, please,' said LeBlanc, 'observe how I scale this deck of playing cards to any seat in the house.' And with a snap of his elbow and wrist, he sailed cards into the auditorium with extraordinary accuracy, landing them in those seats just vacated. The boxes paused, fascinated, as LeBlanc growled to Mignonne and Sing Woo, 'Out the back way.' He continued scaling until his deck was used up, and then he removed his top hat with a bow. 'Owing to unforeseen personnel difficulties, the magic act of the Great LeBlanc has been cancelled.' And with the boxes pursuing him, he joined the others in the wings.

'Through this hall,' said Sing Woo, and they raced down it, and out into the street, where Cocteau and Django joined them.

'Nothing like a dissatisfied audience,' said Django, as the doors of the theater burst open and the boxes rushed out.

'Too late for the Chinese Rice Bowl Illusion,' said Sing Woo. And the united party ran down the street, with the boxes in pursuit.

Argos and the American expatriate saxophonist walked along the boulevard des Italiens; they'd dumped the table they'd stolen, for it was heavy and offered no clue to where Django was except for a few indiscreet images of his affair with Mignonne.

Now they walked past the seven dark entrances to the opera house – sinister eyes watching their march. They passed the Grand Hotel and the office of a steamship company. It was dawn, and Babette and Giselle had said adieu, for daytime was their time for sleeping, but the two musicians kept wandering, Django on their mind.

'We've got to keep pounding the streets,' said the American expatriate saxophonist, 'until something gives.'

'Sure,' said Argos, 'that's all we can do.'

They turned, traced their way back to the boulevard Montmartre. A handsome silver automobile was proceeding toward them rapidly. At the last moment, it screeched over to the curb, and a uniformed driver stepped out and opened the rear door. 'Gentlemen . . .' He extended a gloved hand, indicating the interior.

They climbed into the Rolls, and the driver closed the door briskly behind them. Then he slipped back in behind the wheel, put the car in gear, and continued on down the boulevard.

'There's a picnic basket at your feet, gentlemen.'

They opened it, finding salad, duck, and wine. 'Well, then,' said Argos, 'it's been a while since we've eaten.'

They spread napkins. The driver took them out of the city, in the direction of St-Cloud. Once on the open road, he accelerated, and Argos had difficulty balancing his wine.

'In a hurry?' he asked the driver.

'Orders.'

'From whom?'

'Mr Reinhardt, of course.' The driver pressed the accelerator to the floor, but his gloved hands remained calm at the wheel.

'Hey,' said Argos, 'you're going a hundred and twenty kilometers an hour.'

'I'm trained for these speeds, sir.'

'I'm not.'

'Have some of this duck,' said the American expatriate saxophonist.

Argos picked through the picnic basket. 'Silk napkins . . . champagne . . . say, when did Django hire you?'

'I was only just engaged. It is Mr Reinhardt's desire to have a picnic while traveling at high speed.'

Faster, said a soft, gravelly voice.

'Django!'

They looked around the car, but there was no trace of their partner, only the sound of his guitar playing 'Swinging with Django.'

They sailed on, scattering leaves and much else behind them. The mouth of a tunnel awaited ahead, its stone arch spanning the road, and a cyclist was looking down from its walkway. They entered flying, and the cyclist ran to the other side to see their exit, but he was disappointed, for the sound of the fine Rolls engine faded somewhere within the tunnel.

Argos looked around. Their vehicle was moving along a vast plane of parquet. Their driver was a box.

It was propped up on the seat. A superior and sardonic air was apparent in its movements at the wheel, as the vehicle hurtled along at high speed.

Argos looked at the American expatriate saxophonist. 'Box is driving.'

'So I see.'

Argos leaned forward toward the box. 'Do you know what you're doing?'

The American expatriate saxophonist was looking out the window. 'Since it's managed to get behind the wheel at all, I think we can assume it knows how to drive. Anyway, there's not much around it can run into.'

'This is not St-Cloud,' said Argos.

'No,' said the American expatriate saxophonist, 'we're east of the sun now, Argos.'

'You're perfectly comfortable with a box at the wheel?'

'All right, ask to see his license.'

'I don't want to distract him.'

'Then, relax. We're on a picnic.'

They sat back as the vehicle sped over the plane. They finished the salad, duck, and wine.

'Some kind of forest up ahead,' said Argos.

The American expatriate saxophonist tapped the box on the lid. 'You'd better slow down.'

The box drove full speed into the trees, as Argos and the American expatriate saxophonist dove for the floor. They tumbled over each other as the Rolls bashed into things, careened, skidded around, and straightened. They saw broken umbrellas flying by the windows, and in the next moment found themselves on the floor of Erik Satie's room at Arcueil; the composer was seated on the edge of his chair, in his hat, pince-nez gleaming on the end of his nose as he looked down at them. 'Gentlemen, welcome to my theater for dogs. The curtain goes up. The scenery is a bone.'

The room turned upside down, furniture sliding, and when it righted itself once more, Argos and the American expatriate saxophonist were climbing off the floor of the Rolls, which was still rolling fast. Clinging to its hood and bumper were broken umbrellas, open and flapping like angry crows. The box was at the wheel, with the windshield shattered in front of it.

Argos leaned toward the box. 'Can you see?'

'Does it matter?' said the American expatriate saxophonist, removing bits of the broken picnic basket from around his head. Through the side window, he saw a railroad locomotive, rusted and tangled in vines, and paralyzed on the plain. Clearly, it had been trapped on one of its journeys, perhaps just outside of Paris, perhaps more distant, but it had come to a crossing it had not expected and would move no more.

The Rolls rolled on, past a Paris métro exit, standing alone on the infinite plain. 'Some travelers come out of that,' said Argos, 'and must wonder how they missed their stop.'

In the far distance, crossing the horizon, they saw a caravan of pianos going along on their castors, bright shawls draped over them, fluttering lightly as they moved. The master of the caravan, hunched on the lid of the lead piano, turned to look at the approaching Rolls, and the American expatriate saxophonist saw in the caravan master's slouching form a shape he recognized. 'He's the old piano man. I've been with him in a parlor in a dream somewhere, and it was small and hung with red velvet drapes, and I watched him play, and Argos, what he played was me. And his *technique was flawed*.' The American expatriate saxophonist sank back in his seat, remembering how the old piano man had swayed on the bench, his gray hair shining softly in the light of a candelabrum, his fingers moving, but here and there *faking over it*, and smiling sheepishly.

'Don't let this place get you down,' said Argos.

'And this is where he comes from. He hauls pianos.' The American expatriate saxophonist watched the somber caravan grow smaller, until the old piano man was indistinguishable from the upright on which he rode.

'Nobody's got your final tune in their hands,' said Argos. 'It's yours alone.'

'I remember now – the parlor belonged to Madame des Ricochet. I can see the sunlight on her faded carpet.'

'Those old piano dreams are always around, but you've got to play on through them. Say, listen—' Argos leaned toward the box again. 'Are you taking us to Django?'

A lid opened, and the box offered an assortment of obscene match flaps, playing cards, and risqué views of Paris at night for tourists.

'Try talking to a box,' said Argos, sitting back.

But the city of the boxes was rising up on the horizon, its dark walls glistening with reflected sunlight.

'If we hit that wall it's all over,' said the American expatriate saxophonist. He raised the empty wine bottle in preparation for braining the box and grabbing the wheel, but Argos pointed to the gates opening in the wall.

The box took the Rolls on through, into the city street. All the other boxes turned on their castors, lids flipping open; apparently they'd never seen a Rolls before, or rarely, and now they crowded the street.

'There's some big furniture out there,' said Argos.

'I hear Django's tune more clearly. He must be near.'

'I heard his tune ten years before I met him,' said Argos. 'He could be far down the infinite road.'

'No,' said the American expatriate saxophonist, 'he's in town.'

They pushed open the doors. The boxes crowded in on them. Argos stepped on a hatbox, and from it crawled onto the bigger boxes, walking on their lids, with the American expatriate saxophonist behind him. The boxes were angry, and puzzled, to have the Hot Jazz Duo walking on their flat tops; they tipped backward, trying to ascertain exactly

what was causing these hollow beating sounds.

Argos leapt from a box top onto a low wall, then over it into a back corridor of the city. The American expatriate saxophonist dropped down alongside him. 'What now?'

Argos turned. A candy box was peeking out at them from a doorway.

'Peppermints, caramels, acid drops,' it said, alluringly.

They pushed by it, but the insistent little creature followed them, calling out again, naming the elements of its soul. 'Caramels, fudge, acid drops . . . '

They continued down the back lane of the thorough-fare; other candy boxes, brightly wrapped and painted, called to them softly from doorways. 'I've got a marzipan center, darling, wouldn't you like to try it?'

'How about a nice chocolate-covered cherry, hand-some? Or would you rather divinity fudge?'

'We're looking for a friend,' said Argos.

'I bet you are.'

'Plays the guitar?'

'Nougat's what you want, lovey.'

There were lights burning in rooms nearby. Which of them, wondered Argos, has known Django?

' . . . bonbons, monsieur, honey-coated kisses . . . '

The candy boxes pursued them down the lane, fragile wrappers fluttering, ribbons dangling. A great mirrored wardrobe slid aggressively in front of them, casting an image of the street they were leaving. The image floated out, dividing from itself and casting similar streets in all directions, so that in an instant the musicians were disoriented.

'This way, messieurs,' said the voice of a chocolate box softly. 'Follow your sugar.'

The little heart-shaped box led them through the illusions cast by the wardrobe mirror, and into a narrow hall. It was littered with the tiny skirts of candies and other mementoes of love. The box took them to a doorway leading to another avenue.

'We are in your debt,' said Argos.

'Take me with you,' said the box. 'It's always nice to have candy along.'

The American expatriate saxophonist put the little heart box under his arm.

LeBlanc and his party were themselves surrounded by large, dark boxes at the end of a narrow cul-de-sac into which LeBlanc had led them with great assurances that his intuition could not fail. 'Stuck,' he said, looking at the steep wooden walls surrounding them.

A phalanx of boxes approached them slowly, wheels creaking, legs thumping forward heavily.

'LeBlanc!' cried Mignonne. 'Do something!'

The magician pulled a long clear tube from his sleeve. 'Observe,' he said to the boxes, 'it is transparent and empty. I snap my fingers and—'

Flowers filled the tube, then popped out the end of it toward the boxes, who squeaked and paused, momentarily.

'*Another*,' hissed Mignonne.

'I have in my hand a rope, ladies and gentlemen, a foot in length. My assistant, Mr Woo, will now take an end of it and pull. Observe: the rope is now two feet long. Pull again, Mr Woo . . .'

'They're getting impatient, LeBlanc,' said Django.

' . . . and now you see the rope is four feet long . . . '

The boxes rumbled forward, menacing black, their dark shadows like the ink of a cuttlefish as it spreads in the water.

' . . . now I throw the rope in the air, and behold, it rises to the height of the wall, and remains there.'

Sing Woo and LeBlanc lifted Mignonne onto the rope, and the chanteuse scrambled up it to the top of the wall. 'Come, Monsieur Cocteau . . . ' She reached her hand down, helping the poet upward, and they in turn pulled up Django, Sing Woo, and finally LeBlanc himself.

'That's some trick,' said Django.

'Puchased from the Fakir of Naga,' said LeBlanc, coiling the rope and returning it to his pocket, where it fit without the slightest bulge. 'We used to share a room in Bombay with a cobra.'

Cocteau gazed down on the black shadows hulking below. 'My eyes have adjusted to this place,' he said. 'They are not boxes, they're—'

'Over there!' shouted Django, gazing across the network of streets. 'It's the rest of the Hot Jazz Trio! Boys! Up here!'

Argos and the American expatriate saxophonist looked up, waved, then disappeared into the nearest back alley. In a few moments they were directly below Django, who called for LeBlanc to come with his one-foot rope. The magician lowered it again, down to the musicians, who scrambled up to the rooftop. Cocteau walked to the other end of the roof and looked out over the city, in which he saw the agitation of many box shadows; and he was thinking of a line of poetry by his rival André Breton, a man admittedly tone-deaf. Cocteau spoke it quietly to himself, as he never thought he would.

'I am beginning to see the mean chest of drawers called yesterday gleaming . . .'

And gazing down on the peculiar city, he sensed Breton's presence, but less tangible than flesh, as if Breton were still in bed asleep, connected to the place by the thread of a dream.

'Some furniture is heavier than if it were filled with sand at the bottom of the sea.'

He will write that line this morning when he wakes, thought Cocteau.

'Monsieur Cocteau,' said Mignonne, 'you are standing too close to the edge.' She put her arm through his.

'Yes, thank you, Mignonne . . . ' He turned back, toward the group, huddling now around LeBlanc and Sing Woo.

'We followed Loli's shadow to there—' said Sing Woo, pointing to the intersection of a nearby street. 'Then LeBlanc slipped on a bonbon and went rolling into the gutter like a—'

'Further details won't be necessary, Woo,' said LeBlanc.

He turned to the others. 'Her shadow eluded us, but it may still be close by. We shall have to descend and search. The danger from the boxes is obvious, but our advantage is that they're slow and a little thick-witted.'

'Here, LeBlanc!' shouted Cocteau. 'I've found the trapdoor.' He was pulling on a ring embedded in the wood, a ring also embedded in his dreams, for in sleep he'd done this hundreds of times before, causing the ancient hinges to groan as he lifted the entranceway to a world of still deeper dreaming. He held the trapdoor open now, and the party descended, LeBlanc in the lead.

The staircase was lit by a faint glow from a powdery substance smoldering in little plates placed in niches in the wall. The staircase curved, came out on a landing, and Cocteau recognized the old house on rue La Bruyère, and the hallway along which he'd crept to his grandfather's room.

He entered his grandfather's apartment, went to the closet, and opened it. Within was a green oval box. He lifted the lid and removed a ratty toupee.

'What've you got there?' asked Argos, as Cocteau stepped back out into the hall.

'Rossini's wig. My grandmother used to deliver eggs to him.'

Argos looked at the composer's hairpiece. 'Quite a few tunes in that. But what's it doing here?'

'The boxes read our dreams.'

'Then,' said the American expatriate saxophonist, stepping toward the next door, 'we shall find Madame des Ricochet in here.' He opened the door to Madame's salon. There were numerous mirrors, a fireplace, small lamps, and the walls were hung with plush velvet curtains of faded red. Seated at the piano was the silver-haired caravan master, playing everyone's lives.

'Come on . . . out of it,' said Argos, dragging the American expatriate saxophonist from the room where death awaited him.

'Sooner or later,' said the American expatriate saxophonist.

'Help me with him, Django. He's had a shock along the way.'

They slapped Rossini's wig on his head, and the American expatriate saxophonist's eyes clouded over. 'I hear . . . a cello,' he said in a cracked voice. 'And now . . . I see . . . I grasp the orchestra. Mother sang comic opera in Bologna, you know . . . Sterbini just showed me the most amusing libretto . . . about a barber . . . in Seville . . . '

They continued down the stairs, LeBlanc still in the lead. 'These interiors are fishy, Woo. The whole place is like a loaded hat, if you get what I mean.'

'I looked down the barrel of my assistant's gun,' said Sing Woo. 'It was a wet night in Berlin, and I could hear the faint beating of the raindrops on the roof of the Admirals-Palast. My assistant smiled, pulled the trigger, and a second later I was looking the other way, do you understand? I staggered into the wings, and found myself here, in the land of misfired tricks.'

'A pretty speech, Woo. Now, if you'll stand aside—' But on the next landing LeBlanc was stopped by a figure made of shadows, its eyes the swirling light of distant galaxies.

'What's this?' asked LeBlanc.

'That is Night,' said Woo. 'I wouldn't go near her, if I were you.'

An atmosphere of owls attended Night, but LeBlanc remained confident. 'I can use you,' he said. 'In the Livestock Production Box. After the guinea pig and the rooster, the Shadow of Night. Observe . . .' LeBlanc was moving closer to the shadow, which watched him cautiously with starlit eyes.

LeBlanc signaled Sing Woo to get behind Night, as he continued to distract the figure; from LeBlanc's open palm a golden vase appeared, and out of it then sprang a single night-blooming narcissus.

Night's eyes grew brighter, then gestured in return, and a black drape appeared at the end of her fingers. It hung motionless in the air for a moment, and then she

91

snatched it away, revealing Loli and Bombyx, wrapped in deep embrace, their bodies as if frozen in sleep.

'The living statue trick,' said LeBlanc, grudgingly to Night. 'Very nice. A charming pass. I could get you bookings in the provinces, small clubs at first, and then you work up. Or have you ever thought of playing Upper Poltava? I'm sure your act would look remarkably fresh in the Ukraine.'

A voice issued from the head of Night, distant, as if spoken through a long tube: 'I have already entertained the foreign capitals.'

'Have you? I see—' LeBlanc turned to Woo and said softly, 'I don't like the sound of that. If she comes to Paris with her act, we might as well be swallowing fire on a street corner.'

'Ask her if she does the bullet-catching trick. I've still got my Sturm Ruger Blackhawk with the filed-down plug on the live chamber. If she tries that act, your troubles will be over.'

Night snapped her fingers over Loli and Bombyx and the lovers emerged from the cocoon of enchantment. Bombyx's limp form rippled, twisted awake. 'I dreamt I was human.'

'And I,' said Loli, 'was silk.'

Night, withdrawing, said, 'My starlight wanes, and their dream ends. Who will protect them now?'

'I hear an air,' said the American expatriate saxophonist in Rossini's wig. '*Una voce poco fa* – they are in love. The barber intrigues for them . . . my mother had the greater talent, though Papa was the town trumpeter. But he had to make ends meet as the inspector of slaughterhouses. It made him melancholy. This was in 1792 in Pesaro.'

The door burst open and LeBlanc's Vanishing Box lurched into the room, obviously drunk, eyes crazed with pain. 'Loli, my darling, come back!'

Sing Woo intervened. 'Straighten up there! You're LeBlanc's own box, and obedient to the Cosmopolitan Monarch of Magicians, reserved seats at usual prices.'

'Woo, you're getting to be indispensable.' LeBlanc stepped up to the box and rapped him on the head. 'I happen to have your guarantee in my pocket, from Bartl and Willmann Combined Magical Apparatus Firm of Hamburg.' LeBlanc waved a slip of paper. 'If you insist on carrying on like this, you'll be returned to your makers.'

'Loli, my sweet,' moaned the box, 'my screws are falling out, my drawers are warped. I can't live without you.'

'You have her thrice nightly,' said LeBlanc. 'Why can't you be content with your lot?'

The box opened one of its drawers and took out a pistol. 'She stays with me.'

Loli turned to LeBlanc. 'If I stay, it will be easier for the rest of you. Go without me.'

'Show my assistant her contract, Woo.'

'Sorry, missy,' said Sing Woo. 'The Emperor of Magicians has you sewn up six ways from next Thursday.'

'She belongs to no one but me!' cried the box.

'You sawed-off pile of planks,' hissed LeBlanc, 'I made you what you are.'

The box staggered forward drunkenly, pistol cocked. 'This trick is mine, LeBlanc. I'm in control now.'

'Without me you're a broom closet,' said LeBlanc, snapping an ace below the box's nose. 'You'll be opening and closing thrice nightly for the janitor. Woo, take his firearm.'

'Not me, LeBlanc. I tried that trick one time too many.'

Put on the spot, LeBlanc resorted to more sleight of hand, confusing the box with a release of stage flowers in the face. The box tried to knock them aside, and LeBlanc seized him by the wrist. 'You swine, I'll teach you to threaten my associates.'

The box groaned, pain filling his eyes as LeBlanc twisted his arm behind his back; LeBlanc pressed his advantage, forcing the box to his knees, but a spring-loaded drawer in the back of the box's head shot open and struck the Monarch of Magicians a staggering blow on the bridge of his nose.

Never tussle with the audience, thought LeBlanc, sinking down.

The box tore his arm free, spun toward Loli. 'If I can't have her, no one can!'

With an anguished cry, he fired at the human form he adored. Bombyx streaked in front of Loli, stopping the bullet in the folds of his own body, He fell, red dye spurting from his wound. He looked around in confusion, his voice weak and thin. 'I hear . . . the worms . . . spinning.'

Loli fell to her knees beside him, burying her face in his, and clutching at his limp, streaming fabric. He tried to speak, his voice like the whispering of moth wings. 'Your silk has faded, Loli . . . sooner than we planned.' He became a pure white cloth again, of virgin silk, and the breath was gone from his folds.

Loli spun toward the box, to curse him, but he'd already conjured himself, his humanlike form reverting to its original shape, that of a big, stupid magical cabinet – a Vanishing Box. *This is who he really is*, thought Loli, and found it hard to hate something as dumb as a box.

I succeeded, thought the box.

A hoard of other boxes appeared on the stairs above and thumped down them angrily. LeBlanc and his party backed away, but the stairs themselves opened up, trying to capture them.

'Over the railing!' cried LeBlanc, and they went down his magic rope, to the hallway below, and then out into the street, where more angry boxes thumped and banged. The American expatriate saxophonist in Rossini's wig raised his arm imperiously. 'The chorus is noisy . . . inform them of my arrival.'

'Perhaps,' said Django, 'we should remove the wig.'

'No,' said Argos, 'the raving spirit of Rossini cows the boxes.' It was true: wherever the American expatriate saxophonist in Rossini's wig stepped, the boxes became suddenly docile. Argos and Django shoved the American expatriate saxophonist in Rossini's wig into the lead, and the tumultuous sea of boxes calmed enough to make progress toward the city wall a possibility.

Loli and Mignonne held each other's hands as they ran, and Loli as well held Bombyx, his lifeless body trailing through her fingertips.

But the gates of the city remained closed, the angry boxes milling in front of them. 'You'd think,' said Django, 'we'd stolen their Mona Lisa.'

'Perhaps,' said Cocteau, glancing at Loli, 'we have.'

But then the box of chocolates under the American expatriate saxophonist's arm spoke to the crowd, in her sweet voice, words only another box could understand. Her bonbons poured out, as the American expatriate saxophonist in Rossini's wig waved her around, thinking she was god-knows-what in his delirium. Bonbons bounced off the boxes below, and there was a sound of latches creaking open in response to the little heart-shaped creature in her dainty silver wrapping.

'The gates,' said Mignonne, and pointed. The huge iron hinges were moving.

'Quickly,' said Cocteau, and he led the party through the opening, and out onto the plain, where the statue of Alfreyd O. Montagne Ené de Piro awaited them. 'You are still in danger,' said the statue. 'Do not delay.'

But Cocteau turned back toward the wall. A kite was being flown above the city, a human shape sailing in the wind, arms outstretched, hair blowing, pajamas fluttering, and a string attached to its umbilical region. *Breton* . . .

Cocteau watched the surrealist poet dipping and rising over the city, slippers dangling from his feet.

'What is that?' asked Mignonne, looking at the human kite.

'The hidden heart of a dreamer,' said Cocteau. And lowering his eyes Cocteau saw then the name of the city carved upon its gate – *Astu*.

The others were already moving across the plain, and Cocteau and Mignonne hurried after them, the statue of the unknown figure Alfreyd O. Montagne Ené de Piro shuffling behind. The silver Rolls-Royce, driverless now, came speeding out of the horizon.

'My car!' cried Django. 'You see, Mignonne? I told you I had something nice planned for us.'

The car slowed enough for the party to jump in, with Argos taking the wheel. Django and Mignonne climbed in back, found the empty bottles of wine and the bones of the duck picked clean. 'Some bastards ate our picnic,' said Django, and Argos thought it best not to explain.

A party of marauding silks broke the horizon, sinisterly wrapped nomads on steeds of smoke, armed with gaudy pins. Argos pressed the gas pedal to the floor, and the Rolls shot ahead with the swift silks in pursuit. Rossini's wig blew off the American expatriate saxophonist, allowing him to recover his senses, though bits of operatic overtures popped in and out of his mind as the chase went on.

'Faster!' shouted Django. 'This is my picnic and I must have speed!'

Cocteau and Loli stood on the running board on one side, LeBlanc and Sing Woo stood on the other, as tiny decorative arrows filled the air, fired by the nomads. One struck a tire, slowly deflating it, but Argos rode on the rim; another of the tiny arrows pierced Cocteau's neck, and he heard the voice of his supposed friend, Coco Chanel, saying, 'Cocteau? An insect! An *amusing* insect, if you will.' He pulled the little arrow from his wound, and threw it away, but the insult remained in his bloodstream.

Sing Woo turned on the running board, drew his Sturm Ruger Blackhawk, and fired on their pursuers. One of the nomads shrieked, fell backward in his saddle, and hung limp as his horse of smoke raced on.

'Good shooting, Woo!' shouted LeBlanc.

'Magical and Philosophical Illusions Nightly,' said Sing Woo, and fired again.

'Faster!' shouted Django, poking Argos on the shoulder.

'I've got it to the floor, Django.'

'There's the métro stop ahead,' said the American expatriate saxophonist. Argos turned the wheel and sped the Rolls toward the glowing glass balls of the station.

'Don't stop till we land in a ditch!' ordered Django.

Argos ignored this injunction and quite sensibly brought the Rolls to a stop at the métro entrance. Cocteau led the way down the stairs. The statue of Alfreyd O. Montagne Ené de Piro was waiting on the platform, but when the crowd of hurtling Parisian artists hurried up beside him, he pretended not to know them. The light of the train appeared, and then its roaring filled the tunnel. The party got on, all except for Sing Woo, who seemed to have run into an impenetrable barrier at the doorway of the train.

'LeBlanc!'

'Come on, Woo,' said LeBlanc, grabbing Sing Woo's sleeve.

'It's no good. I can never take this train. I've tried before.' The Chinese conjuror turned toward the staircase and raised his revolver. 'I'll hold them off.' He fired and dozens of doves filled the platform, Sing Woo dis-appearing behind the veil of their fluttering wings.

'He had only one good trick,' said LeBlanc, peering through the window as the train pulled out, 'but I'm going to miss him.'

The train rattled on, through the tunnel. The party chattered excitedly, except for LeBlanc, who was thinking about the irrepressible Woo he'd see no more, unless he tried the bullet-catching trick himself. Beside him, Loli clutched the dead handkerchief that had been Bombyx.

'Odéon,' said Argos, as the train pulled into its next stop.

The party got off, except for Alfreyd O. Montagne Ené de Piro, who remained in the métro car; a moment later the mysterious figure was taken away by the train, on into the tunnel, toward other rendezvous.

In his tiny room, on his tiny bed piled high with books, Cocteau sat staring out the window toward the garden. Surrounding him were masks of many kinds, whose

empty eyes stared with him toward the window. He sat smoking, a cigarette held between his long thin fingers. He tapped the ash into his palm, then absentmindedly scattered it to the floor.

'Astu,' he said, aloud, gazing out the window.

And in the place de l'Opéra, at the Café Certa, Paris headquarters of Dada, André Breton was seated at a table writing the same four letters, over and over, in preparation for dissolving them into the waters of a poem. Yet he had to return to Astu numerous times throughout the years before this was done, flying, as always, in his bedroom slippers, on the end of a midnight kite string.

The Hot Jazz Trio played a tune called 'Parfum,' and Django's guitar sang nights of a Gypsy's Paris, and nights of rectangular conjuration, and no one in the nightclub crowd knew exactly how he did it, not even Mignonne. When his strings caused the drunks near the bar to sway, Mignonne swayed too – the tune's promise just beyond reach. Where had Django come from, and where would he go? He left hotels in only his hat.

As for the American expatriate saxophonist, it was noticed that the strains of Rossini crept into his runs.

Argos whacked his bass and talked to it as he played: We're blown to the winds eventually, but for now, for now we have brought Django back from the Land of Boxes . . .

. . . while in another part of the town, LeBlanc was causing Loli to levitate in her harem costume, pots of incense burning at her head and feet. Sewn into the gaudy pattern that covered her bosom was a small square of white silk. 'Now, ladies and gentlemen, as she floats there in trance, I shall pass this hoop around her, so you may be assured there is nothing supporting her here . . . or here . . . thank you very much . . .'

The curtain fell, and Loli and LeBlanc returned to the wings. 'Not a bad house tonight,' said LeBlanc.

'Are we never going to use the Vanishing Box again?'

'The Great LeBlanc hasn't got time for any more rescue expeditions. Come on, curtain call.'

They went back out, bowed once again, and then proceeded down the hallway to their dressing room. There the Vanishing Box sat, occupying a corner of the room, and when Loli appeared a slight squeak came from it, but LeBlanc had chained it shut, and fastened it with a padlock.

'It's lonely,' said Loli, whose memory of recent events was a dyed dream, colors blending one into the other, leaving her with only a feeling of having been adored, and it had begun with this box.

'Don't go near it.' LeBlanc sat down at his mirror and renewed his makeup. 'I've written to the manufacturer for an explanation.'

'The explanation is love.'

'Not for LeBlanc, Monarch of Magicians. There's a flaw in that box somewhere. I'll have an answer from Hamburg within the week, or strong measures will be taken.' LeBlanc brushed his mustache with a tiny comb and studied the effect in the mirror. 'Reputations are at stake.'

'Poor box,' said Loli, stroking its face.

'Don't encourage the brute.'

A sudden rapping sounded from within the box. LeBlanc turned in his chair. 'I told you to leave it alone.'

'But listen—' said Loli. The rapping increased, and the box began to rock back and forth, a muffled voice calling from within it, '*LeBlanc . . .*'

'I've had enough of this,' said LeBlanc, rising from his chair and charging at the box. 'Shut up!' He shoved it with both hands, deeper into the corner, but the box rocked back out, the muffled voice continuing to call from within it, '*LeBlanc, let me out . . .*'

'That's odd,' said LeBlanc. 'It sounded like . . .' He removed the key from his vest, opened the padlock, and swung open the door.

Sing Woo stumbled out, pigtail waving, arms flailing. 'Thank goodness . . . you heard me . . .'

'Brandy, Loli . . . Woo, my dear old chap . . . here, drink this . . .'

But Woo was tearing open his mandarin's jacket in order to look down at the bullet hole in his chest; he appeared greatly relieved to find it plugged up.

LeBlanc peered at the wound. 'Stuffed with something, is it?'

'A bonbon.' Sing Woo passed a hand across his sweating brow. 'I've been through a lot, LeBlanc.'

'I dare say you have.'

'I solved the bullet-catching trick the hard way.' The Oriental magician slumped down on a chair. 'I'll have to get a broadsider printed up, The Return of Sing Woo from the Dead. Do you think I can get bookings again?'

'I'd temper the announcements slightly. Bound to be trouble if you go too far. The Return of Sing Woo should be sufficient.'

'But LeBlanc, I've done it. I've come back.'

'And we're all delighted.'

Sing Woo turned toward the Vanishing Box. 'That's the key to it all.'

'Yes, and I've written a stern letter to Bartl and Willmann about it.'

'I'll buy it from you, LeBlanc. Name your price.'

'Throw in with me, Woo. Equal billing, and the box is yours free and clear, until I hear from Hamburg.'

'I've been away, LeBlanc. Except for this raising-the-dead trick, my repertoire is rusty.'

'Woo, there comes a time in a magician's life when he must share what he has, within limits, of course.'

They shook hands, and Loli closed the box, murmuring to it softly as the two magicians toasted their new act.

'To the pack of cards.'

They drank, and Loli tightened the chain and secured the lock.

I did it all for you, Loww-leee, whispered the box.

Blues
on the Nile
A Fragment of Papyrus

'And how long will you be staying in our Tomb City, Majesty?' asked the Chief Architect.

'We must leave tomorrow,' said Pharaoh, sucking spiced beer through a straw. 'A thousand tasks await me.'

The Pharaoh's Chief Praiser hiccuped silently, then spoke from his place at the banquet table. 'His Majesty's work is never done, his works are many and profound. This is our Leader, our Chief, without defect, sublime in his intent—'

The Chief Praiser's solemn incantation ceased as the dancing girls entered the party room and began their Moon Configurations, each girl representing one phase of the night jewel. Punctuating the sound of their ankle bells came the distant sound of the whip, cracking even in the night, over the heads of the slaveworkers toiling in the City of Pharaoh's Tomb.

'We've made great progress since your last visit, Sire,' said the Chief Architect, nodding toward the whip sounds.

'He has given us slaves,' chanted the Chief Praiser. 'Thousands has he smote and put in chains. This is our ruler, provided with flames, far-reaching of hand, generous, astute, wise as the sun, purified in his nest—'

'Purified in my nest?' Pharaoh lifted his eyebrow.

'It is an accepted laudation, Your Majesty,' said the Chief Praiser, putting on a wounded expression.

Pharaoh shook his head, indicating wonder, but the Chief Praiser was allowed to continue. His chanting was drowned out, however, by the cackling laughter of Pharaoh's dwarf, who ran among the dancing girls, swinging a toy mummy on the end of a string and making lewd comments. The delicate Moon Configurations were spoiled, the dancing girls tripping and squealing as they were struck by the mummy.

'What a disgusting little man,' said the Chief Architect's wife. 'If I may say so, Your Majesty.'

'Oh yes, quite,' said Pharaoh. 'Quite disgusting.' Pharaoh sat back in his seat, his shoulder stiff from bow practice. He rubbed it gingerly, and the Chief Praiser, seeing the soreness, rushed to incorporate it in his litany.

'Master of the compound bow, suffering to learn all martial arts in the protection of his people . . . '

The Chief Praiser rose from his seat, slightly drunk, and feeling the winds of inspiration whirling him upward. Attempting to forge one of the great chains of praise, he waved his arms outward over Pharaoh's head.

' . . . Lord of the Solar Barque, a cloud of divinity, a never-setting star, who never sinned, the bull of terror to his foe, who possesses all things, quicker than the greyhound, soul of mankind, who rescued our kingdom in times of violence, who has destroyed evil, who . . . '

The Chief Praiser fell into a fatal pause, but started up again quickly. '. . . who is the double Lion God, who throws excrement in the face of his enemies, who never stole milk from a child—'

'That will do for now, Chief Praiser. Rest yourself.' Pharaoh turned to the Chief Architect and said quietly, 'He's good for about an hour of solid praise and then he starts grasping at straws.' Pharaoh reached for his beer, and the pain in his right arm struck again, down the length of it and across his chest.

'Are you ill, Sire?'

'No, but tell me, who is that guest there? I do not recognize him from my own ranks.' Pharaoh pointed to a tall man in a white robe, whose manners were perfect, who spoke to no one, who placed a cup to his lips.

'Which man, Your Majesty?'

'There, he turns toward me. He wears a red stone at his throat. '

The Chief Architect cast his gaze where Pharaoh's finger pointed. 'But I see no such man, Majesty.'

'He carries a papyrus roll. How strange his skin is – he's been burned at the neck. Observe, Architect, if you have eyes in your head, his skin is like a reptile's.'

'Sire . . . ' The Chief Architect's face filled with concern. He signaled the Fan Bearers to increase the air currents about the Pharaoh's brow.

'You don't see the noble lord approaching me?' asked Pharaoh, staring straight at the man, who was now but a few feet from the banquet table, a faint smile on his lips.

'No, Sire.'

Pharaoh looked quickly to his dwarf, who stood mouth open, eyes wide in terror, his gaze where Pharaoh's was.

'What do you see!' snapped the Ruler.

'A shadow,' answered the dwarf. He turned, running away on his deformed legs, dragging his little mummy behind him.

'So,' said Pharaoh, rising to receive the honored guest.

'I must touch you, Majesty,' said the guest.

Pharaoh extended his hand, and the guest's leathery finger touched him lightly. An enormous stone fell from the firmament, and Pharaoh felt its cold edge crushing his chest. The banquet room dimmed. His doctors were surrounding him. The honored guest was leaving, through a rear door, past the spear-holding guards.

A second slab of granite fell, filling the pores of Pharaoh's body with stone, and the banquet room was no longer visible. Instead, Pharaoh dimly beheld the interior of his great tomb, and saw his gathered people, and heard his final praises being sung.

' . . . this was our Great King, the Perfect Cleansed One, who has gone to his horizon . . . '

The Chief Praiser spoke, and the two lands were filled with crying.

' . . . he goes up the smoke of the great exhalation. Mighty in life, he is thousandfold mighty in death. Discernment is placed at his feet. He has captured the horizon. We, his willing servants go with him, into darkness, with the prayer that we may join him on his voyage, upon the Solar Barque.'

Pharaoh saw his dwarf being dragged to the tomb, heels digging in against the sand, but the dwarf was no match for the soldiers, and they hurled him into the crypt. The Chief Praiser and the Chief Praiser's wife entered of their own accord, and then a third slab of stone came down on Pharaoh's soul, settling into place with a sound that reverberated endlessly, a thousand thunders echoing across the sky.

Pharaoh was entombed.

Out of the dark density of the night stone, he perceived a ray of light growing ever brighter and more splendid. It dissolved the hard edges of the stone, turning the stone to dark water. The heaviness that had surrounded and crushed him became a warm bath.

He stood upon the shore of a black Nile.

There was no palace, no houses, no fields of waving grain.

There was a black Nile and a golden ship.

The ship came slowly over the water; strange and beautiful lights emanated from the hull, sweeping the surface of the black Nile.

Pharaoh waited on the shore as the ship came near, and all was in stillness except for the lapping of the black waves. The ship sent forth a white beam of light that crossed the water and touched the shore at his feet.

He stepped upon it and found it firm enough to hold his spirit-body.

The ship was deserted, moving under a mysterious and silent power. Pharaoh wandered the decks, which were made of a finely woven substance, luminous and pulsating. While studying its peculiarities, he discovered that his own body was made of the same substance – a dancing light of gold with a fringe of emerald green.

Entering the captain's cabin he found it luxuriously appointed but deserted. The ship nonetheless kept a straight course over the dark waters. As the furnishings of the boat were first-class, he felt that all was proceeding according to divine plan and that he, as the Son of

Heaven, would soon reach his eternal home. He relaxed upon a soft white couch and watched the dark shore flow by.

To his surprise, another craft appeared out of the darkness – a tiny canoe, primitive in the extreme. What was such a vulgar vessel doing on the divine waterway? Pharaoh walked out on deck to investigate. Leaning against the rail, he peered out across the water and discovered that it was his dwarf in the canoe, furiously paddling.

Pharaoh attempted a greeting and found that his mouth was closed tight. He strained to open it but could not. He waved his arms, trying to attract the dwarf's attention, for the little fellow would be amusing to have on board.

The dwarf saw the signal, stopped paddling for a moment, and stared at Pharaoh. Pharaoh gave another commanding wave.

The dwarf answered with an obscene gesture and resumed paddling, off down a dark, silent tributary.

Pharaoh stood dumbfounded at the rail.

I gave him the finest tomb in the world, and he gives me insult. Should we meet again in this dark world I'll pay the pygmy back, or I'm not the All Gracious One.

Pharaoh, still puzzling about the ingratitude of slaves, found a flight of stairs leading to a galley of the boat. He descended them, attracted by the aroma of cooking soup. Following his nose, he opened a door and was astounded to see the Chief Praiser and his wife inside, at the stove, cooking supper.

'Your Majesty, how wonderful to see you again!' The Chief Praiser leapt up, praising and bowing. 'We're honored, honored. Please be seated, O ruler of nations, O sanctified dispenser of happiness.'

Pharaoh pointed to his mouth which he could not open.

'Your mouth is closed up, Majesty? But of course, of course. Sire, please let me open it for you. I found the instrument our first night on board.'

The Chief Praiser went to the corner of the galley and brought forth a piece of wood shaped into a ram's head, crowned by a snake. 'If you'll allow me, Sire . . . '

The Chief Praiser placed the snake's head on the lips of Pharaoh and pried them open, along with his teeth. 'There you are, Highness. *The dead shall speak,* as the saying goes, only a matter of finding the right tool.'

'How came you and your wife to be aboard my solar craft?' asked Pharaoh, not unkindly, for he was grateful to the Chief Praiser for that little trick of opening the mouth.

'Your craft, Majesty?' The Chief Praiser looked puzzled.

'Yes,' said Pharaoh. 'I'm merely curious, Chief Praiser. Believe me when I say I'm happy to have you on board my eternal ship.'

'Your Majesty is joking, as always,' said the Chief Praiser. 'Your tongue is subtle, swift, speaks in riddling wonders, has a thousand currents, is never tired—'

'Chief Praiser, an answer, please.'

'Majesty, there is some small misunderstanding, mine of course. I cannot follow your lightning-fast implications, cannot discern the delicacy of your reasoning. I can only say that this humble craft is the spiritual property of my wife and me. There, as you can see, upon the walls is written the history of our life. You'll find it upon this wall and all the walls. This poor ship bears all the traces of our time on earth, Majesty, where we served humbly in your magnificent court.' The Chief Praiser scraped, bowed a little, and concluded: 'In no way could this simple ship be called your Solar Barque, Majesty. Such a thing is laughable. Your solar craft is made of blinding light, is filled with magical garlands, is attended by countless goddesses. *Isis and Nephthys salute thee, they sing unto thee in thy boat hymns of joy.* You're the ruler of the gods, Majesty, and your boat is beyond description.' The Chief Praiser rapped the cupboard of the galley. 'We have here a sturdy vessel, a good little craft, but a Solar Barque? Never, Majesty, never.'

Pharaoh reflected over this peculiar turn of events, then

113

turned to the walls of the galley where the inscriptions were written in glowing azure letters. Indeed, they did describe the life of the Chief Praiser and his wife. So must the inscriptions on deck, which he'd seen on first boarding but hadn't bothered to read, for he was accustomed to thinking that all such inscriptions naturally referred to his own glorious self.

Where then, he asked himself quietly, is my boat? Did I miss it?

He turned to the Chief Praiser. 'Yes, of course, Chief Praiser, as you say, your boat indeed. And a fine boat it is. I wanted to extend my blessing to it, wanted to sanctify it with my presence, in gratitude for the wonderful service you gave me all through life.'

'I'm deeply touched, Majesty,' said the Chief Praiser, fawning slightly as he laid out two golden soup bowls. 'We have here a soup of some delicacy, if you'd care to join me.'

'Happy to, Chief Praiser, happy,' said Pharaoh, who, now that his mouth was open, saw no reason not to fill it. He sat down at the emerald table and tucked a napkin under his chin. 'You didn't happen to actually . . . see the Solar Barque around anywhere, did you?'

'No, Majesty, I didn't.' The Chief Praiser ladled out the soup with a golden spoon. 'There's no trouble with it, is there, Sire?'

'No, no, certainly not. I was just wondering – what you thought of it, how you liked the style. She's a magnificent boat, makes wonderful time. I sent it on ahead when I saw your boat. I said to Isis, there's the Chief Praiser's boat, and I wish to travel in it, for the Chief Praiser is the finest of men.'

'Majesty, there are tears of joy in my eyes, and in those of my wife.'

The Chief Praiser's wife lowered her head, her eyes appearing to be filled not with joy, but with hunger.

'Your wife is very silent, Chief Praiser. Is there some trouble?'

The Chief Praiser spooned soup to his lips. 'She's still

115

upset over being suffocated in your tomb, and as I'd rather not listen to her complaints, Your Majesty, I haven't opened her mouth. If you know what's good for you, Sire, you will allow the situation to remain so.'

Pharoah spent the voyage walking on deck with the Chief Praiser, or snoozing in the empty guest room. The heavenly soup was continually replenished in a mysterious way.

'One of the features on a spiritual boat,' said the Praiser. 'I suppose they do it much more grandly on the Solar Barque.'

'Actually,' said Pharaoh nervously, 'I prefer the simple fare of your boat.'

'You are a man of the people, Majesty. It is your greatness and your glory. I shall praise this aspect of your nature throughout eternity.'

Pharaoh signaled an end to the discussion, for references to the Solar Barque put the All Gracious One on edge. It wouldn't do for the Chief Praiser to know that his sovereign was nothing but a stowaway. This entire affair, reflected Pharaoh, is typical of the oversight one encounters at the higher levels of government. When he met with the Divine Hierarchy, he'd set some heads rolling.

Thus did they sail on, until they discerned a light in the distance, growing slowly brighter as they approached. The entire river was finally lit with its majestic fire, the celestial radiance of the spiritual sun, toward which many craft were sailing, to Judgment Day, in the Hall of Truth.

'They weigh one's heart in the scale,' said the Chief Praiser. 'But of course that's just a mere formality for you. As for her—' He pointed at his wife. 'I don't know. She frequently lapsed into inattentiveness when I practiced my praising.'

His wife's mute face grew fearful. She reached into her robe and brought out her heart – a tiny red vase, which she held up to them.

The Chief Praiser laughed scornfully, reached into his own robe, and came out with a dented coin, which he held up to the spiritual sun. 'Catches the light nicely, don't you think? Well, in any case, our hearts don't matter, Your Majesty, for we are merely part of your entourage. Your great and glorious heart will gain us our admittance.'

'Yes, certainly,' said Pharaoh. 'To be sure . . . ' The sovereign excused himself then, explaining that he wanted to take one last walk around deck before they docked. When he was out of sight behind the wheel house, he reached inside his robe. His hand passed through layers of golden weave, which kept parting before him, ever opening. He rummaged around, fished and searched, then tore the robe off and shook it.

'There must be . . . some sort of mistake . . . '

He turned the robe inside out, held it up to the light, examined the sleeves, the cuffs, the lining.

But he found no heart. Thus prepared for judgment, he watched somewhat uneasily as the boat docked, and a crocodile-headed god motioned him down the gangplank.

Boxcar Blues

Melrose rode his unicycle and I followed in my clown car. It crashed and I popped out the top on a spring-loaded seat, which is how I billed myself – Poppo the Clown. This was with the General Lopez Circus, that traveled all over the country, with winter quarters in the poorhouse.

General Lopez's whip was cracking and Melrose and me scrambled up the balance pole. We clowned there, fifty feet above the ground, the pole swaying back and forth. Balance is a fine line, you might say. When you got it you are floating, when you lose it you are through.

I was looking down at the crowd, and that is when I saw seated in the front row a gentleman in a suit made of fish scales, shining in the circus light. His hair was slicked-down black, and his face was pale white. I says to myself, *Who sold a ticket to Death?*

Next thing I know, the pole is cracking, I hear it like my own spine snapping, and then Melrose and me are falling through the air and we hit that circus floor with a dull thud and a puff of straw.

We came to at night in a hospital, and I had a pin in my collarbone and Melrose had a bandage around his head. When the nurse came by, we asked her where the circus was and she said, 'Well, it's gone. But you boys have a visitor. I'll send him in.'

I looked down the hall and saw Death waiting on a bench in his fish-skin cloak. The nurse smiled at him and pointed toward our door.

'Come on, Melrose,' I said, and we bailed out the window.

'Yes,' said Melrose, 'we've got to catch General Lopez, for there aren't many clown jobs to be had.'

We got out of town, heading for the river. Near the riverbank we saw the flickering of a campfire. We gave a hullo and stepped into the firelight. A grizzled old tramp looked at us. 'Soup Kitchen Salamancus is the name. This here is the Dipper.' He pointed his thumb at the hobo beside him, a giant with shoulders like a buffalo.

'We been on the tramp a while,' said Soup Kitchen. 'I'm form'ly an orthopedic surgeon, the Dipper was an astronaut.'

Next morning we took an old railroad bridge across the river. 'The women in this town are down on men who are cheerful,' said Soup Kitchen as we hit the street. 'You got to give them a sad story.'

He went to a back door and knocked, explaining through the screen how he'd been with the biggest brokerage firm in the country and lost it all overnight. A stern-looking woman peered back at us from the hall, and Melrose whipped out his juggler's balls and set them whirling. This softened her and she let us chop wood and stack it in the yard, and next thing you know we were looking at tea and little cakes. 'Tell me of the misery you've faced on the road,' she said. 'Wring my heart with it.'

'Once I had it all,' said Soup Kitchen, 'crystal goblets with my name in them and the fam'ly coat of arms. My watch was a gold coin. Look at me now.' He flapped his toothless gums.

'And you?' asked the woman, looking at Dipper.

'Form'ly I was a minister of God. I had divine guidance and two Cadillacs. Now I ain't fit for nothin' but trash.' He wrung his two big meat hooks, and a tear trickled down along his bulbous nose. Tears came into the woman's eyes too, and she nodded her head toward the radio.

'I believe I heard you on the air.'

'More'n likely.'

We ate the cakes and when nothing more seemed forthcoming we excused ourselves. 'Where are you poor men headed for?' she asked, stepping with us into the backyard.

'For ruination, likely,' said Soup Kitchen.

I saw that woman's shadow then, falling on the yard, and the edges gleamed with sudden light, like a black cloak trimmed with fish scales.

'The yard needs work,' she said. 'We'll plant a row of violets. I'm all alone here.' Her voice was even and low. I felt that dull thud again in the back of my head and said to Melrose, 'I can't balance this, let's go.' He nodded and we cleared out of there. When we were halfway down the block, Soup Kitchen turned around and said, 'That's strange, ain't it? She's standin' there still as a statue. A bird could light on 'er.'

'One of them stone women,' said Dipper. And we kept on going.

Soup Kitchen knew the railroads, and we hopped a freight going west, in pursuit of General Lopez's circus. At night, while we rolled, an apparition huddled with us. 'Diesel-fire eyes,' said Soup Kitchen.

I carry cargo, said the spirit. *All manner of things.*

That singsong spirit voice put a chill on me. *I carry all they give me, my rails run straight.*

'A boxcar ghost,' said the Dipper.

The souls of men are all the same to me, my doors shut tight, next stop eternity.

The spirit started fading, and Soup Kitchen said, 'Train whistles blend when they pass each other. Weird bein's are born.'

Dipper uncorked some homemade booze, and Melrose grew thoughtful. 'There's a bareback rider named Lulu talked French to her horse. I seem to see her now, in her little white costume.'

'I've loved fancy women meself,' said Soup Kitchen. He ran a leathery hand over his stubbled chin. 'In the days when I had it all.'

'What days were them?' asked Dipper.

'You ain't seen everything, son,' said Soup Kitchen. 'Imagine me in a tall hat and pointed shoes.'

The train whistle blew, and from afar another whistle answered, and that boxcar ghost floated in again, in tall hat and pointed shoes, swinging a polished cane. It had Soup Kitchen's face, looking forty years younger. A gold watch chain hung across his vest and he was walking down the avenue of his dreams.

Come next sunup we were on the outskirts of another town. When the train slowed, Soup Kitchen jumped, his ratty coat splaying out around him, his toothless mouth set in a concentrated look as he landed and continued on in a low running crouch until he had his balance. Melrose and me sailed out after him, and for a moment I felt the General Lopez Circus, and knew it had just preceded us. We turned, and the Dipper was in the door of the freight, big as a backhoe. He hunched over and dropped; a cloud of dust surrounded him as his great shoes slapped the earth.

I went down into a ditch beside the road, to the mouth of a big tin culvert. A little trickle of water came out. I put my head inside and gave a whisper. *General Lopez, this is Poppo. Me and Melrose are taggin' right along.* The whisper flew in a spiral, echoing out the other end, and I saw the center ring shining, and a whip cracked in my ear.

'She's a good sleep in there when she's dry.' Soup Kitchen was peering in beside me, as the circus ring faded. 'When she's wet, you can't get worse, a man takes a chill he'll never lose.'

Above the culvert, I saw the tattered edges of a circus poster hung on a crumbling wall. The date on the poster was ten years old. Melrose stepped in beside me, staring at that familiar red border, but the painted letters had all faded, along with the tiger's face.

'That's your circus, boys?' Soup Kitchen squinted at the poster. 'Looks like she's been gone for some while.'

We walked on, but me and Melrose kept glancing over

our shoulder at that washed-out poster. Soup Kitchen noticed and, looking straight ahead, said, 'Don't worry 'bout time.'

We made our way to the riverbank and soon we had a frypan crackling in front of us. Our backs were against a pile of old railroad ties, and we caught sight of a snake in there, wriggling against the wood to get its old skin off. When the snake freed itself from its worn-out suit, Melrose grabbed the empty skin and studied it for a long time.

'Toss 'er in the pan,' said Soup Kitchen, 'she'll be just like tortilla chips.' But the Dipper claimed it for his portable still. The skin disappeared into the bubbling mash and he swirled it around, stirring deeply.

Soup Kitchen returned to his frypan and served us a stack of the queerest tasting pancakes I'd ever had. 'These are Peoria Pollencakes,' he said, sliding one on my plate. 'Spices and whatnot.'

The Dipper was frowning as he chewed. 'You still ain't got the recipeet right.'

'You think I don't know how to make Peoria Pollencakes? That recipeet was given to me on a man's deathbed.'

'So long as he didn't die from eating them,' said Melrose. 'Tastes like—' He closed his eyes. '—like something I had once, quite a while back.'

'Well, of course Peoria Pollencakes goes back a long ways,' said Soup Kitchen.

We sat there on the shoreline, dreaming out over the water. When I caught a glimpse of Soup Kitchen's face, I saw a road map written on it, through the state of Idaho, at Horseshoe Bend outside of Boise, a town we'd once played.

'I saw a butlerfly once,' said Dipper. 'A big one, fastened tight to the deck of a ship. Hangin' on with her wings all tattered and blowin'. Now that butlerfly was hitchin' a ride across the Great Lakes, you can't tell me different.'

'It weren't no Great Lakes.' Soup Kitchen pointed his chin toward the field rushing past us. 'It were the big divide.'

Melrose's eyes flashed an acrobat's look that sees through space, judging it exactly. For a moment I felt myself falling with tattered wings, and the dull thud sounded in my brain like a drum, and the eyes of the tigers flamed up.

'But I made a mistake that day,' said the Dipper. 'I catched that butlerfly in a bottle. I figured I'd make the crossing easier for her.'

'There's always some damn fool around, ain't there,' said Soup Kitchen quietly, up through his hat.

'And when we docked I took the bottle out on shore and let that butlerfly go—' Dipper mimed an open bottle in his hands, which he shook in the air, out toward the field beyond us. 'She was a sorry sight, floppin' on the dock. I innerfered with her mermentum.' Dipper crackled his huge knuckles. 'And things ain't been right with me since that day.'

'Thing've never been right with you, you dadblamed idjut,' said Soup Kitchen under his hat.

When evening came on, we made our way to a gin mill on the edge of town. 'Sometimes I get lonely on the road,' said Dipper, as we entered. 'I get to almost cryin'. If I could just get tied up with some old whore, life would be sweeter'n honey.'

'Don't get into your blubberin',' said Soup Kitchen.

'That's a tender barfly,' said Dipper quietly, pointing to a heavyset woman at the bar. She wore a blond wig, a silver satin jacket, and faded jeans that spread around her big hips. Dipper walked to the bar and moved onto the stool beside her. The bartender called her Pearl and was lighting her cigarette. She let twin streams of smoke out of her nose and looked at Dipper. 'Haven't seen you around here before.'

'Ain't been here before.'

'You work at the Bottle Exchange?'

'Can't say I do.'

'Thought I saw you there.'

'I'm from the circus,' said Dipper with a wink toward

127

me. 'We got some hootchy-kootchy ladies not half so sassy as you, whyn't you give it a try? I could arrange a special tryout.'

'I'm too wide in the behind for a grass skirt.'

'There are men with a dollar and a half in their pocket would fight to see you, Pearl.'

'A dollar and a half? Why, you buffalo, I'm cashier in the best hotel this town's got, with a fancy restaurant attached.'

'We got a tent pegged by the river,' said Dipper. 'Whyn't you join the party? I've brewed some of the best booze a cashier ever tasted.'

Pearl opened her purse and applied a touch of powder to her cheek. 'I only date executives.'

'Stick with us, girlie,' said Soup Kitchen. 'We know how to make a lady comfor'ble.'

'I'll bet you do,' said Pearl, looking down at his sawed-off, wrinkled form. Pearl had a few more drinks, but when no executives showed up, she said she'd show us a place that was pretty in the moonlight.

We followed her to an old backstop on a rugged ballfield. 'There used to be some mighty ballplayers passed through here,' she said. 'They're just shadows now.'

We watched the shadows play – old-time ballplayers battling each other, pasting the moonball, and spirit-sliding into second in deep silence.

'I was an infielder meself,' said Soup Kitchen.

'The only thing you ever fielded was a potato,' said Pearl. She crossed her legs and smoothed the knees of her jeans. The Dipper was on the ground in front of her. 'You're a great beauty, a real looker.'

She sat back, a tin cup of his hooch at her lips. 'A lovely summer night. I don't get outdoors enough.'

'Throw in with us, Pearl,' said the Dipper. 'You're tired of this town, ain't you?'

'Don't get so personal. Where were you brought up, in a gopher hole?'

Melrose was gliding away to the edge of the trees.

His clothes came off and we saw his naked body for a moment, before he stepped into darkness with a snaking move.

'They'll arrest him for that,' said Pearl.

I went to tend Melrose and found him rolling around on the ground in a patch of moonlight. A forked tongue flickered over his lips, and his body snapped. He sprang to his feet and a thin membrane peeled from his torso. He wriggled again and it came loose and he held it at arm's length.

'I done it, Poppo.'

It dangled from his hand, transparent and limp, with moonlight shining through it as if it were a piece of the moon's own robe. It was a clown's light, deceptive and foolish. He folded it up and handed it to me while he dressed. It breathed gently in my palms, and little points of moonlight beamed from it. 'Melrose, do you remember that old clown Bobby used to be with the show? Had a shadow of black cloth followed him on the end of a string? I'm now inclined to believe it wasn't black cloth.'

'No, it weren't,' said Melrose, 'and there wasn't no string.'

We walked back along to our camp in left field. Suddenly a pair of headlights lit the baseline, and Pearl said, 'Cops, it's a good thing you've got your pants on.' She led us to a cowpath in back of the ballfield, and we followed it while the cops rolled on by. Soup Kitchen watched their taillights vanish in the dark. 'Some night them two fellers'll be just a memory. Ain't that right, Dipper?'

'Yes,' said Dipper, 'they'll be old men in their beds.'

Soup Kitchen's eyes crinkled at the corners, his face like an old lizard's. 'And we'll still be out here travelin'.'

We followed the cowpath to an embankment overlooking the railroad yard. One of the yard men was moving through with his lantern, from track to track. We were hidden in the shadows, but he turned toward us anyway and looked up. His lantern raised slowly near his face. His hair was slicked-down black and his face was moon white and I saw his cloak and fish-scale collar. 'We can't go down there,' I said to Soup Kitchen.

Death signaled us with his lantern, waving it back and forth, and then withdrew into the darkness of the yard.

'She's clear, Poppo,' said Soup Kitchen. 'Some of these brakemen give a tramp a hand.'

'That was no brakeman,' said Melrose.

'I says the way is clear,' snapped Soup Kitchen. 'You think I don't know who's who on this line?'

We followed him down the tracks, but Pearl was not enthusiastic. 'I'm not riding in any boxcar,' she said, but the Dipper picked her up by the waist and set her in the doorway of a car.

'Oh Lord,' groaned Pearl, as we climbed up beside her, 'this is what comes of getting tanked with strangers.'

The freight gave a little jerk and we were moving. Pearl shook her head, perplexed at what was happening to the woman who ran the cash register at the hotel. 'I'm tanked up now,' she said, 'but oh my god, tomorrow—'

Melrose opened his palm and the moonshine was shining in it. He shook it out and the skin dangled, half alive, from his hand.

'Now what in hell is that?' asked Pearl.

'Just a clown act,' said Melrose softly. 'I control it with a string.' He flicked his wrist and the moonskin danced around the boxcar. It tumbled and floated, soft lights swirling inside it, and Pearl said she could see exactly how the string worked it.

I saw General Lopez fill out the floating form, his silver hair gleaming, his white tuxedo shining with rhinestones. Pearl sat on a piece of cardboard, hands around her knees, watching the darkness rush past. ' . . . on a freight train with these bozos, Pearl, Pearl, what have you done?'

'This is one of them cars with encased ball bearin's,'

131

said Soup Kitchen to her as she bounced on the boxcar floor. 'Rides smooth as a porcupine in your butt.'

The night sky was cloudless and I saw a comet, and General Lopez whispered, *The comets are acrobats, Poppo, they are the best. That is where our circus has gone.*

I felt my own silvery skin itching me, and rubbed my back against the boxcar door.

'You buggers don't have lice too?' Pearl moved away and I was suddenly staring at my own silver moonskin floating above me.

'Grab it, Poppo,' said Melrose, 'before it departs.'

I slipped my arm into it, and it spread, becoming a satiny cape, which glowed around me. I reflected on Bobby the Clown, whose cloak had been a black shadow dancing elusively under the Big Top. And I saw that the lining of my cloak was black satin. I whipped it outward, and knew that I was a piece of the darkness.

The mind of General Lopez enfolded me, as if he were this cloak, a mixture of arc light and magic. I heard his snapping whip, and I snapped the cloak again, flashing it silvery, then black, at Melrose.

'Yes, Poppo,' he said, 'so I see.' He flipped his own moonskin, and now two circus shadows danced in the boxcar, tiptoeing around in silhouette. The shadows were quick, faster than ordinary ones, as if a flicker ahead of perception.

One of them stepped in Soup Kitchen's hat, and he looked out from under it. 'Take them kites over a ways, will you, boys, I'm gettin' some shuteye.'

Melrose and me practiced with the satin silhouettes through the night, as Dipper and Pearl fell asleep on the boxcar floor, Pearl's sandals half off and a puzzled expression on her dreaming face.

Where am I bound for with these deadbeats? wondered Pearl. She'd awakened in the night. *I'm an educated woman, able to do figures in my head.* 'Hey—' She shook Dipper awake. 'I don't take to being kidnapped.'

133

'You're pretty as a butlerfly,' said Dipper, and wings spread out behind him – big gorgeous things of gold and black, with velvet tips. They fanned slowly back and forth at her, and Dipper's face changed too, his eyes a myriad of tiny lenses, like an insect monarch.

'You're not as ugly as I thought,' said Pearl.

We woke in a train yard, Pearl unfolding herself from Dipper's arms. The butterfly wings of the night had vanished, and she was looking at Dipper's unshaven face. 'Ohmygod,' she said, as her whereabouts came clear to her, that she was nowhere with a bunch of bums.

Soup Kitchen led us through the dusty yard, and I could smell the ghost of our circus, for we'd traveled by rail often enough and unloaded at dawn. But the traces of the whole world are in a railroad yard at sunrise, when the brakemen's voices echo far up the tracks.

We ate then, and stretched out to relax, but Pearl wouldn't let it be. 'You've got to ship me back. I'm due for work.'

'That job's long gone,' said Melrose quietly. His eyes met hers, reptile cold, and I saw a shiver go up Pearl's back. I walked down to the stream to wash and saw another campfire, with a figure hunched over it, facing the river. He was a solitary tramp, closed up in himself. But I gave him a hail anyway, and he looked at me, and it was my turn to shiver.

That fish-skin face, silvery scaled, and those cavernous eyes – Death knew his way through these jungles all right. 'Poppo,' he said, 'you and I must talk.'

That underwater voice had hooks in it, barbed and impossible to escape, and I trembled on the sands of that riverbank as Death smiled. But then I remembered my silvery form, the skin I'd shed, and I flicked it in the air. The skin danced and Death watched it, as I slowly backed away.

I backed into Melrose, pointed, and said, 'We've got to get clear of here.'

'Reel in your moonskin, Poppo,' said Melrose. 'You don't want to lose that.'

'I'll shed another,' I said, and left Death to claim it.

Soup Kitchen came down, a pot in his hand, and went straight to the river, where he and Death knelt at the water, jawing. I saw those fearful fish scales flash as Death smiled at Soup Kitchen, and then Soup Kitchen waved his pot in the wind to dry it, and came back up the hill. 'Feller down there says we can make a west-bound freight inside the hour.'

'You know him?' I asked.

'Oh, he rides this line now and again.'

We grabbed that westbound freight, lifting Pearl up on the run. She moaned and groaned but we got her aboard. She stared out at the passing station yard. 'I'm in a boxcar again.'

'The world is just rollin' freight, Pearl,' said Soup Kitchen. 'But you know that.'

'I don't want any of your happy hobo horeshit,' said Pearl.

Dipper was in the corner of the car, drawing clear drops of liquid from his still. 'She's fetchin' up.'

'You don't know nothin' about stills,' said Soup Kitchen. 'Now old Henry Potato, there was a traveler knew how to make good booze.'

'Henry Potato? He never tasted anythin' this good.'

'Yes, well you don't see him ridin' no more. And do you know why? Because he transmogr'fied himself, is why. He found where the rails meet.'

'I heard he just fell off a trestle.'

'You hear one thing and another.'

'I've been abducted,' said Pearl, touching at her big bouffant.

Her makeup had run and she had circles under her eyes. One of Melrose's little snake scales had landed on her cheek like a diamond tear, and she looked the next thing to a sad clown, and I tried to cheer her up. 'We lost our circus, Pearl, but we're catching up.

135

You'll find your cash register too.'

'I might have wound up working in a casino at Atlantic City. I'd made some connections. Certain gentlemen were interested.' She touched at her wig again.

'I know they were, Pearl.'

'No, you don't know anything about a refined life. I don't mean to be harsh, but you're just a carnie. I used to know businessmen.'

'General Lopez did a good business in the east.'

'How old a man is he?' Pearl touched at her eye makeup.

'Age unknown. But he understands wild animals.'

'You see? Who's interested in wild animals? I was associated with a number of sales representatives who came regularly to the hotel – gentlemen who had every major credit card.'

'They could not crack a whip like General Lopez.'

'They weren't runnin' a menagerie act. They were corporate figures.' She sighed again and looked out the door. 'There's no future in a boxcar with a bunch of clowns.'

I touched her shoulder gently. 'You have a circus woman's heart, Pearl. You're gutsy.'

'Oh, get lost,' she said, and took to brooding again, about the miles, I suppose.

I grabbed the ladder beside the door, climbed to the roof of the car, and saw Melrose sitting there, staring into the distance. 'I'll tell you this, Poppo, we never were who we thought. We were other travelers, hidden in the midst of things familiar.'

When the sun was gone, Pearl mellowed some and began talking about different guests of distinction who'd stayed at the hotel where she'd been employed. 'There was one gentleman of foreign extraction, who wore a beautiful cloak and had very fine manners. They said he was a count, and he was most attentive to me.' Pearl looked around at us accusingly. 'I was hoping to meet him, when you losers showed up.'

136

'Did he have a moon-pale face, Pearl?'

'His skin was delicate.'

'And did his eyes make you think of caves lit from deep inside?'

'He had a piercing glance. It went right through me. They said he was an importer.'

'Export, Pearl. He handles out-going freight.' We'd have to keep her with us or she'd be labeled and shipped where she would not want to go. I looked out and saw Death, trying to shunt us down his own track toward a skull-shaped mountain of ice.

'He's late,' said Soup Kitchen. 'Out drinkin' last night and lost some silver at the poker table too.'

We picked up steam, rolled on by, and left him there in the yard, staring after us.

A tear trickled out of Pearl's eye. 'I feel this train's got me.'

'It's just a dumb beast,' said Soup Kitchen, 'but it's home.'

'Home? I had a fluffy bathrobe on a hook. I had a boudoir chair with satin tufts.'

'I got tufts grow'n' out my ears,' said Soup Kitchen.

Melrose shook his moonskin and shaped it into a tiny juggler, who worked on the tip of his finger, juggling little silver balls.

'What is this?' I asked, for the paths of the little balls were wonderful to watch.

'These here—' He nodded to the balls dancing on his fingertips. '—are *life*.' He spun around, and his body became a thin silhouette, one side bright silver balls, the other flat black, and the whole thing no thicker than a leaf. He twirled, and beads and shadow showed in sequence, first one, then the other, faster and faster.

'I knowed a hobo had a similar penchant for display,' said Soup Kitchen, as he stared at Melrose's spinning form. 'Roundhouse Roy was his name, and that bum could spin.'

Melrose spun off into the corner of the boxcar, and Soup Kitchen walked over to the door, where he stood, watching the sun go down. He pointed into the scrub pines, and I saw the flash of a camp there, and shadowy forms around it in ancient armor. Soup Kitchen turned to me. 'Trampin' is what them old knights do nowadays. You meet them on the line now and again. Their talk is not like yours and mine, Poppo.'

I stood at the door, watching their forest tableau disappearing, until only a tiny flicker of fire was left and then it too was gone. 'How long have you been riding, Soup Kitchen?'

His toothless mouth broke into a grin, and the twilight laid mild gold on his brow, as if it had known him long and was protective of the old tramp at evening. His shabby figure became burnished before me, and I felt him merging with invisible elements. It lasted only a moment and then Soup Kitchen's gold was gone. 'Now comes the owl moon,' he said.

The train steamed on into darkness, but after a while she began to slow. 'We'll ride on through,' said Soup Kitchen. 'This town we're headin' into don't have a soul.'

'But it has a phone,' said Pearl, and poised herself at the edge of the car. When it slowed to a stop, she jumped down and stamped off across the tracks. As she neared the platform, a pale light shone on her, giving an icy translucency to her hair.

'Now we'll have to get her back,' said Soup Kitchen. We followed him through the yard, into town. Main Street seemed familiar. 'Have we played this town, Melrose?'

'You never played this town,' said Soup Kitchen. 'This town is playin' you.' He pointed to successive streets appearing, jewel-lit, the town growing larger with every step we took.

'Listen,' I said, 'I hear circus music!'

'T'aint real, Poppo. It's a see-duction. When a town don't have no soul, you got to watch out. Now we'll find Pearl at a big hotel, and it'll be just the one for her.'

We hunted out the biggest hotel in town, and Pearl was

there, working the cash register at the restaurant.

'Don't bother me,' she said, 'I've found my kind of work.'

'Come on, Pearl,' said Soup Kitchen, 'we've got a train to catch.'

'Get out of here,' hissed Pearl. 'This is a respectable place.'

The hotel clerk looked our way, a frown on his face. Soup Kitchen spread his coattails out like a fan and danced around the lobby, cackling. He jumped on the plush sofas with his boots, then swung on the glass chandelier, dragging the thing down to the floor with him. The crystal shattered and then melted away to water on the floor. 'There she goes,' he said, 'that's the beginnin'.'

The entire hotel grew translucent – and then began to melt. In a few minutes we were standing in the desert under an empty sky, and there were no streets, no lights, no town at all.

'You little runt,' said Pearl. 'You've ruined a fine hotel.'

'Come along, girlie,' said Soup Kitchen, and he led us back through the desert to the station yard. The lanterns of the signalmen were still making slow arcs in the air, but I saw now that they too were fading. 'They're the last to go,' said Soup Kitchen, and by the time we climbed back into the boxcar the yard was dark as a grave.

'I had a good job there,' said Pearl.

'You was food for the coyotes,' said Soup Kitchen. 'This town's their makin'. They'da et you right off your mahogany stool.'

We looked out then, and saw the eyes of the pack shining all along the track. 'Coyote magic, see, but if you ride this line long enough you can handle it.'

Dipper was approaching Pearl again, with love in his eyes. 'Pearl, you ever made a bed out of thousand-mile paper?' He pointed to a pile of heavy brown paper, one side of which was covered with tar. 'It makes good insulation.' He began to work with an old packing crate, hammering it around and spreading the paper out in thin layers. He worked in shadows, but now and again when the train turned a bend, the moonlight broke through to the corner and we saw a silver satin bed, fluffy and cushioned and softly shining, like the bed of a movie queen or some other flamboyant lady. 'I'm workin' on 'er, Pearl. Just you be patient.'

Pearl stood with us in the doorway, and Soup Kitchen nodded back toward Dipper's corner. 'He's a simple-minded feller, but you could do worse.'

'I find that hard to imagine.' Pearl kept her gaze on the darkness rushing past us and began speaking softly, as if to herself. 'I had all my savings in wigs, and they were beautiful things.'

'I bet they were, Pearl,' said Soup Kitchen. 'You're the kind of woman can wear one.'

'And I had other lovely things too.'

'Sech as—'

'A nice little apartment, a pop toaster.'

Soup Kitchen raised his hat up and down. 'Light, medium, and dark.'

'Oh, leave me alone.'

'The night is long, girlie, ain't you heard? People got to speak to one 'nuther.'

'I'm an abducted woman.'

'Pearl—' Dipper called as the moonlight struck his corner, and we turned and saw a canopy of silver around a lunar bed of satin. 'I put in the stuff you like,' he said, pointing to a little footstool and matching boudoir chair.

'I'm not some Boxcar Betty,' she said, putting one hand stubbornly to her hip.

The Dipper approached her slowly. 'These here thousand-mile-paper moon beds last all night, Pearl. So whenever you get tired, you just go and stretch yourself out and no one will bother you.'

'Pull the other one.'

'I'm just a tramp, Pearl, but I ain't never forced my attentions on nobody.'

Dipper fell back into the shadows; a gurgling sound came from his distillery.

'You drove a poor man to drink,' said Soup Kitchen.

'It was a short drive,' said Pearl. She gazed at us, mistrust and distaste in her eyes. But I could see she was weary, and she said, 'I'm going to sleep now and I don't want any funny business.'

She walked over to the corner where her satin moon bed waited, and as she approached, it glowed more brightly, for the moon was keeping pace with us through the open door. She slipped out of her sandals and climbed into it, fluffing out her wig on the pillow. The moon fell behind a cloud and Pearl and her bed were darkened, but not before I saw a monarch's wings emerge from the sheets beside her.

Next day we saw the mountains, and by nightfall we were beginning a long slow climb into them. Soup Kitchen announced that we were bailing out and promptly went off the side, landing in his scuttling crouch. We followed him to a clearing, where we made a cook-fire. Dipper passed tin cups of moonshine around, and Soup Kitchen drained his with a choking little gasp. 'Give me room—' He began a hobo dance, his battered pants flapping, his coattails spread out like a bat's wings. Little twittering sounds came from his beard.

'He'll take right off any minute,' said the Dipper to Pearl.

'You think I care? He can turn himself inside out, but it won't bring back my career.'

A snapping sound filled the clearing as Soup Kitchen turned himself inside out, his body a red rubbery color and his bones illuminated. 'How'zat, girlie,' said a muffled voice from somewhere in his head.

Pearl had her nose in the air, a hard woman to impress. Soup Kitchen snapped back to his outer form and continued his shuffling dance around the fire.

Dipper underwent a fierce struggle in himself, brow furrowed in the firelight, and I saw his butterfly wings emerge and then fold around him in the shape of a

conservative business suit, from which he looked at Pearl with a cheesy smile.

' . . . called you here to co'nordinate the latest sales figgers.' He gestured as at a conference table, but Pearl pushed him away, and his suit vanished, wings fluttering downward in despair.

I heard General Lopez in the wind, blowing his ringmaster's whistle. *Poppo, he whispered, don't be afraid of the future.*

'General,' I answered, 'me and Melrose are out here on the bum, trying to locate you.'

I am standing before you, he said, and appeared in a band of moonlight. *The troupe awaits you.* His whip cracked and he vanished.

But what came from the darkness then was a birdheaded man, crowned with feathers of luminous green. He pointed at Melrose and me. 'These souls belong to the underworld.' His voice was a bird's, and I knew he was a regent of Death.

'Pay 'im no mind, Poppo.' Soup Kitchen moved toward the bird-headed regent. 'G'wan, you stuffed turkey, 'fore I sharpen my knife on you.' He crouched, then leapt in a long, graceful glide, over the fire and toward the regent, coattails fluttering wildly. The regent drew back, protesting. 'Intervention is not allowed.'

Soup Kitchen snapped his coattails again, emitting tongues of fire he'd gathered into them. The bird-headed man withdrew to the shadows, and returned with Death himself – the spectator of the circus show, face glistening with fish scales.

'I've got a bus waiting for you boys.'

'Lissen, Count,' said Soup Kitchen, 'these are just some tramps been travelin' this line for years. You're tappin' the wrong fellers.'

'Here are the stubs,' said Death, holding up two torn tickets from the show. 'They fell from a fifty-foot pole.'

'We're only talkin' dorsal vertebrae.'

'We're talking broken neck,' said Death.

'Tell you what,' said Soup Kitchen, digging in his

143

pocket, 'let's roll bones for the boys.'

Death smiled, the fish scales glistening on his fingertips. 'You know my weakness.'

Soup Kitchen shook the dice, muttering to them and shuffling around in a little dance. Then he began his windup, gyrating wildly, his arms cranking up and down in spastic violent motions. The dice flew in the darkness, struck, and rolled toward Death's feet. Twin beams of light shot from his eyes, illuminating the bones.

Soup Kitchen whooped. 'Holy old seven! So long, Count.' He scooped up the dice and put them back in his pocket.

'You have bought time,' said Death, still smiling, unruffled by his loss. 'Do you know how many time-buyers I have met? Do you know how many I have on account? It matters little,' he said indifferently, and nodded to his regent. 'We shall withdraw.'

'Death is a sport,' said Soup Kitchen, as the two figures stepped back into the shadows. 'Many's the 'bo knows that.'

'What did he mean – we're on account?'

'It'll do you no good to reflect on sech things. Rejoice in the moonlight, boys.'

Melrose looked at Soup Kitchen. 'You know that fish-skinned devil can't be beat.'

'He's been beat for now,' said Soup Kitchen. 'Has any pore fool got more?'

We felt the city coming at us, a big city of the West, and the railroad yard was a massive labyrinth through which we snaked, cars creaking and screeching as they swayed from side to side. Patterns came and went in the tracks, iron alphabets, X's and Y's shunting us along. My life could have been otherwise, if the X had been a Y when the first carnival came to town and a clown taught me to juggle. I'd been lured by motion, and then by freakish women.

'We'll go to the professional area,' said Soup Kitchen

as we lowered down. 'Mix with the advertising crowd on their lunch hour.' He flapped his baggy pants. 'They might hire me on for a washday commercial.'

We followed him out of the yard, into the iron city. Stone lions, belching water, guarded a public square. And I thought, who can ever find us here? This city is full of time-buyers, with all kinds of long-term arrangements.

The sun beat on the square, and waves of heat shimmered in the air. Pearl sat on the fountain's edge. 'This town'll have the job I want.'

'This town's not for you, Pearl. The overtime will wreck your disposition.'

'I'll have to get some clothes,' said Pearl, touching at her wig. 'A cashier has to look like something.'

'You look like the moon of the prairie.' A butterfly was fluttering above the crowd and over the fountain, and Dipper studied its flight as it beat its wings above the spray. A tiny clicking noise escaped his lips, and the insect hovered near his head, then landed in his hair. He turned to show Pearl, but she was watching the crowd.

The figures who passed us were established in this dimension, and the sunlight shone for them, and the shadows were their own. But we were estranged, the sunlight like a metallic vapor.

'Soup Kitchen,' I said, 'what has happened?'

'We shifted to another track,' said Soup Kitchen. 'You got to accept the loss of cities and much else besides.'

I saw a tattered piece of a circus poster, blown along by the wind, with a tiger's face upon it, one familiar to me. It blew on by, and vanished up the avenue, announcing the past.

Soup Kitchen was staring into the fountain's play. How long had he ridden these rails that lead to cities populated by alien beings?

Only the large carp swimming lazily in the fountain seemed interested in our presence. One of them came

146

to my fingertips, and a bubble formed on its lips. It floated to the surface, its delicate orb shimmering prismatically. 'Poppo,' it said softly, as it burst. I looked across the fountain and saw the fish-scaled body of Death moving toward us through the crowd.

'Soup Kitchen,' I said, 'our time's run out.'

'The matter's serious, boys.' He moved away from the fountain, and we moved with him. The pavement was white with sunlight, a blinding day in the city, unrelieved.

'Melrose,' I said, 'I've known this moment before.'

'You've known it all your days,' muttered Soup Kitchen.

Dipper and Pearl hurried beside us, Pearl protesting, but Dipper kept her moving. 'Hey,' said Pearl, 'I'm not on wheels, y'know.'

'You're a good girl, Pearl, but you're slow.'

'I lie in bed on Sunday and look at my wigs. That's the kind of person I am.' She turned around. 'Why, there's the gentleman I was hoping to meet when you slugs came along. He's my importer. Darling—' She waved. 'Here I am.'

Melrose and me grabbed her by the elbows and dragged her forward. 'Pearl, that rube is not for you.'

She protested, kicking her legs and stamping the ground. 'How would you know? How could you know about the arrangements people in business make?'

Death was bowing to her, in his most genteel fashion.

'He's a big operator,' said Pearl, 'and he's interested in me. It could change my whole future. Don't you understand?'

'Pearl—' Death's smooth voice was calling to her through the crowd. '—we're going to have an expense account dinner.'

'He's everything I ever wanted,' said Pearl.

Soup Kitchen laughed with a choking little cough that racked him as we ran, and Death's body gleamed with the sun's reflected brilliance, his scales an impenetrable armor. The bird-headed regent had joined him now, and they hurried after us through the crowd.

But then I heard the music of our circus, and it slowed my step. Melrose stopped too, for the music promised all vanished things would return. But Soup Kitchen rammed us with a lowered shoulder and sent us pitching forward. 'The winds in this town are clever. They practice on man's hopes.'

'Then why did we come here?'

'Poppo, it don't matter where we come. We rendezvous jest the same.'

And the city, its pillars burnished with harsh bronze light, received us without hiding us. A van, bearing a politician's blaring loudspeaker, went past, calling its demons to worship. 'He'll git my vote,' said Soup Kitchen, removing his hat with a flourish, then hurrying on, hat jammed back down on his head.

Death was still flirting with Pearl, an embossed briefcase in his hand as he waved. 'Pearl, you'll help me go over my accounts.'

'He needs me.' Pearl kicked Melrose in the ankle and broke my grip, but the Dipper picked her up in his massive arms and rushed forward with her. Death's regent, perhaps sensing an oportunity to advance in the corporation, made a rush at us, crowing officiously for us to stop. A circus clown is not taken in by that sort of fool. I flipped three balls toward him with a subtle spin; his hands had to follow their orbit, and the balls controlled him, set him juggling as he stumbled along. But Death intervened, and was a master juggler; he moved the balls easily, and his touch set them flaming. They burned in his hand, to ashes, and he tossed the ashes away; they made a circus sound in the wind that blew them on.

The streets of the city had widened, and factory buildings lined them, with tramps sleeping in doorways. Wine bottles lay scattered around, broken and empty, and drunken figures wove along the avenue, muttering songs and life stories to the bricks. 'Dear Christ, I'm on skid row,' groaned Pearl.

Here the beings were no longer alien, but creatures

149

like ourselves, balanced on a bit mournful laughter. Soup Kitchen waved to an old derelict on a crutch. 'Boys, Pearl, this is Gumbo Joe.'

Gumbo Joe lifted his filthy cap to Pearl. 'Pleased to make yer acquaint'nance, I'm sure.'

Pearl stepped back, wiping her hands nervously on her jeans as she looked around for a taxi; but a bum was working the street with a rag, and the only cab in sight swerved down another block to avoid having its windshield greased.

'The Fish is after us,' said Soup Kitchen to Gumbo Joe, who nodded, saying, 'I don't mind him s'much as that buzzard he brangs with him.'

'We're lookin' to part company from both,' said Soup Kitchen. 'These boys fell off the balance pole, y'see.' He pointed to Melrose and me, and Melrose drew out his silver shadow and set it dancing on the glass-littered avenue.

'Now that's a pretty thing,' said Gumbo Joe, and began dancing with it, thumping his crutch. Something quivered within me and my own silvery sheath slipped out, joining the dance.

Gumbo Joe roused the other tramps of the avenue, and they staggered around, shouting wild cries into the air, half-truths and women's names. Death and his regent stared, transfixed by the grotesque gathering.

Pearl was trying to flag cars in the street, but Dipper turned her toward him. His monarch's wings unfolded, white gold in the sunlight of the city. His eyes changed into clusters of diamonds; then jewels dotted his body all over, and his wings creaked with tiny clicking noises, as if he were a mechanical pin from a royal house. 'I'm richer'n any salesman, Pearl. I can give you wigs made by the swallers in spring.'

'I can't build security on skid row,' said Pearl, looking at the mad-eyed bums throwing empty bottles and trash at Death.

Dipper fanned his wings and stepped toward her, antennae of faceted gems flickering out of his forehead.

'I'm your very own butlerfly, Pearl. Your jewel bug of joy.'

'I want the simple things,' said Pearl. 'You'll never understand.' She stood before him, fists balled on her hips. 'A new electric stove and a self-defrosting fridge. What do you know about things like that?'

'I know the stars and the moonlight, Pearl,' said Dipper, desperately. 'I can talk to bees.'

'If you were a beekeeper, it might be useful.' Pearl fluffed out the locks on her wig and drew a long strand down in front of her eyes. 'This thing is filthy.'

'I'll clean 'er for you, Pearl,' said the great mechanical butterfly. 'This stuff cuts grease like nothin' you ever seen.' He held out a flask of his moonshine, but a tramp grabbed it from him and drank it back with a yell. 'Thunderation! That's some medicine you got there, Johnny.'

We retreated while the bums held back Death with their volley of oaths. A bottle struck the regent in the head and he sank to the pave. Gumbo Joe swung his crutch in the air and Melrose's silvery-beaded shadow whirled with mine, approaching Death slowly. His fish eyes were not perfect on land, he might mistake our shadows for ourselves. The silver silhouettes glided in front of him, performing a balance routine that was the soul of our act; glittering, smooth as mercury, they tumbled for him, and he paused, squinting. Then his arm lashed out, and he brushed them violently aside; they collapsed, and their sequined forms fell apart, snake scales blowing away with a hissing sound. 'Poppo and Melrose,' said Death, gazing toward us. but the winos let off another volley of empty bottles. Gumbo Joe waved his crutch and gave a whoop. 'That's it, boys! Hold to 'er! Flail 'em with cabbage!' He pranced and hobbled, a maniacal grin on his face, one tooth showing in the center of his mouth. 'We're too bent for ye!' He waved his crutch at Death. 'We're indestruct'nable.'

Death threaded his way slowly through the debris, with the drunken men still taunting him, threatening to filet

151

him. Death's gaze did not falter and his manner remained calm. He had no hostility, no ire.

A ragged old wino stepped from a doorway and swayed before Death, brandishing a bottle. 'C'mon, gimme yer best shot.'

Death flicked a finger, and the wino shuddered and fell forward, stiffening all over. Gumbo Joe leapt in and knelt over the fallen man. 'You killed Big Nose Bob!'

'Yes, the schedule permitted it. Big Nose Bob will take a special bus tonight.'

'I'm the King of the Tramps,' snarled Gumbo Joe. 'And I don't take kindly to this.'

'I'm the King of Darkness,' said Death, 'and you are much the same as the rest.'

'We'll see 'bout that.' Gumbo Joe drew a small bottle from his pocket and held it up to the sun. The cork popped out, followed by a swirling cloud. 'You ain't never seen a rig like this, for I got it from Wanderin' John, and it's the pure breath of trampin'.' Gumbo Joe laughed as the cloud mist began to glow with an inner light. 'And Wanderin' John got it from Solomon the Wise, you know that bum, I believe,' he said, turning to Soup Kitchen.

'Know 'im well.'

'And Solomon the Wise got it from Little River Eddie who some say was three-quarter Cherokee.'

'That story's been tolt.'

'And the substernce in this bottle *has* been fetched up correct.'

Gumbo Joe looked at Dipper, who scrutinized it carefully, big wings slowly fanning. 'So that's how she's done.'

'You better believe that's how she's done,' said Gumbo Joe, holding the bottle higher, as the last of the fragrant mist poured out of it. 'And a man can make do with it, can make hisself whole and indestruct'nable, and Death ner any other fish can take him.' Gumbo Joe turned to me and Melrose. 'Take 'er, boys. You're friends of Soup Kitchen's and you're friends of mine.'

Melrose gazed at the undulating mist, then turned to

152

Gumbo Joe and said quietly, 'We can't take a man's last drop of medicine.'

'Take 'er,' said Gumbo Joe, 'while I'm in the mood.'

'Excuse me,' said Death, 'but Wandering John's head is on the coatrack in my hall. And his mist was of no use to him when I called, though he spread it quite thickly in the air. So if you gentlemen will just cooperate—'

'You're bluffin', you weasel. Wanderin' John and Little River Eddie are free. They escaped you, and these boys are goin' to escape you.' Gumbo Joe waved us toward the mist. 'C'mon, git in, git in, you too, Soup Kitchen, I know your ticket's been punched.'

The shadow of huge monarch wings showed beside us, slowly fanning, and Soup Kitchen said to Gumbo Joe, 'I cain't leave the Dipper and his girl.'

Dipper's voice came in a crackling rasp, but I couldn't understand his words; his great golden wings pushed me and Melrose and Soup Kitchen into the mist. It gathered quickly around us and I knew it was an atmosphere in which Death couldn't breathe; but I saw him conferring with Gumbo Joe, and heard him say, 'Then it must be you, my friend, as I think you know.'

'That's as it goes,' said Gumbo Joe.

'Gumbo!' cried Soup Kitchen, trying to push back out of the mist, but the breath of that world outside would no longer admit him and he sagged back into the swirling wisps that surrounded us.

Through the mist, I saw Gumbo Joe holding Death back with his crutch, still taunting him, but Death knocked it aside and harsh metallic light leapt from Death's eyes. Gumbo Joe fell, his fingers grasping feebly toward the mist. 'Little River Eddie give it to Solomon the Wise . . . and Solomon give it to Wanderin' John who give it to me . . . and I give it to some pals . . . make shore you git that down in your book.'

'It has been duly noted,' said Death, and I strained to hear more, but the mist was thickening around us, and I felt the plates of the world shifting.

'Nobody believed he were King of the Tramps,' muttered Soup Kitchen. 'Now I'll have to find him in shadows and repay my debt.'

Kings don't need no pay, Soup Kitchen, said Gumbo Joe's voice in the air.

The mist was changing; it made a crackling sound and solidified into glass. I looked down and saw it under my feet, thick and almost opaque, with a trademark in it.

'A bottle,' said Melrose, banging the glass wall before us. 'We're inside a bottle.'

A huge label advertised a wino's cheap Tokay. Beyond the edge of the label, through the glass walls, I saw only blue space.

'Is she corked, that's the question,' said Soup Kitchen, craning his head backward. 'If so, we'll have to pop 'er, for I don't fancy spendin' my old age in here.'

We lifted him on our shoulders and he crawled up into the neck of the bottle, bracing his feet on both sides. He pushed himself higher, and then called back down to us. 'Clear away, boys!'

We scaled the bottle's neck, and popped out beside him on the rim. Soup Kitchen shook his head with a laugh. 'Did you ever hear that old hobo tune, "I went to Turkey on a Bottle"? I've long reflected on its meanin' and it now appears I have understood.'

All around us was the boundless sky. From the blue expanse, several small brilliant lights appeared, and as they approached us I saw these lights were dangling like diamonds on the end of glistening strings strung high into heaven. The lights grew brighter, the strings became silver ropes, and we saw diamond-suited acrobats swinging on them in immense arcs through space. As the silvery ropes whipped near us, the acrobats let go and sailed on, floating freely, their expressions remote, their faces concentrated in celestial thought.

'The circus of General Lopez travels farther than we dreamed, Melrose,' I said, as we watched the acrobats glide on in their astounding, infinite arc. They tumbled slowly, in their bright beautiful costumes, off into the

155

immensity of distances. Their ropes swung back empty, and Soup Kitchen steered the neck of our bottle toward them. As the ropes came nearer, I saw they were woven of light, a pulsing elegant weave.

'Don't be bashful, boys,' said Soup Kitchen, and holding his hat, he grabbed one of the ropes and floated off on it.

Melrose leapt and I followed, the two of us clinging to the other rope, our fingers merging with the light in an unbreakable grip. The rope hurled us backward in a long, slow arc. I turned and saw Gumbo Joe's great floating bottle turning to mist again, changing to a man-shaped cloud; this being grew more distinct, and carried a hobo's pack on his back, made of the same swirling mist. His giant figure turned toward us, and he waved a misty, wrinkled cap. His eyes were pools of whirling fog. 'The true form of the breath of trampin',' said Soup Kitchen softly, waving back as the cloud figure moved on over the edge of the world.

Our ropes reached the end of their arc and then reversed themselves, swinging us in the direction the other acrobats had taken. A strand of light separated from the rope and twined itself around me like a bright, rippling snake, and a moment later it had covered me in a diamond suit such as the others had worn. Melrose underwent the same costume change, and I knew that this had always been our profession, and all other endeavors a dream upon the balance pole. There was only this – the eternity of the tumblers. I turned to Soup Kitchen gliding beside us, expecting to see him costumed and gleaming, but he was still in his baggy pants and patchwork jacket; his rope was gaining in velocity, and as it whipped far forward he let go, floating off it and spreading his jacket like a flying squirrel. His eyes were closed, and his toothless gums clamped in a smile of glory.

I released my grip and floated beside him, and then Melrose was floating beside me, the three of us gliding in perfect freedom out in the endless fields of blue, the sublime motion filling me with thoughts a clown seldom has.

'Tis a shame though,' said Soup Kitchen, opening his

157

eyes, 'that we had to leave Pearl and Dipper behind.'

Melrose pointed, and we saw just below us a monarch's wings, tattered and ragged from a difficult flight; and in the monarch's arms was a big woman in a golden wig that was long and streaming as the sunlight.

'I'll try it for a while,' she was saying, 'but don't go getting any ideas.'

'Pearl of the sun,' said the Dipper, scattering gold dust from his tattered wings before her as they climbed. 'Pearl of a pore bum's dreams.'

'Well, the wig fits nice,' she admitted, and brushed it out behind her as she glided, her fingers running through its sun-dancing texture.

'In the far reaches of the ages,' said Melrose, 'we will reach a ring past which none can go. It is the end of the world.'

'We'll slip through 'er,' said Soup Kitchen. 'I seen fences like that round the B&O yards. You cain't let sech things hold you back when you're on the bum.'

'We shall see,' said Melrose.

''Deed we shall,' said Soup Kitchen.

And we tumbled on.

A SELECTED LIST OF FINE NOVELS
AVAILABLE FROM BLACK SWAN

☐	99075 2	QUEEN LUCIA	E.F. Benson	£4.99
☐	99076 0	LUCIA IN LONDON	E.F. Benson	£4.99
☐	99083 3	MISS MAPP	E.F. Benson	£4.99
☐	99084 1	MAPP AND LUCIA	E.F. Benson	£4.99
☐	99087 6	LUCIA'S PROGRESS	E.F. Benson	£4.99
☐	99088 4	TROUBLE FOR LUCIA	E.F. Benson	£4.99
☐	99202 X	LUCIA IN WARTIME	Tom Holt	£4.99
☐	99281 X	LUCIA TRIUMPHANT	Tom Holt	£4.99
☐	99348 4	SUCKING SHERBERT LEMONS	Michael Carson	£4.99
☐	99169 4	GOD KNOWS	Joseph Heller	£3.95
☐	99195 3	CATCH-22	Joseph Heller	£5.99
☐	99208 9	THE 158LB MARRIAGE	John Irving	£4.99
☐	99204 6	THE CIDER HOUSE RULES	John Irving	£5.99
☐	99209 7	THE HOTEL NEW HAMPSHIRE	John Irving	£6.99
☐	99369 7	A PRAYER FOR OWEN HEANY	John Irving	£5.99
☐	99206 2	SETTING FREE THE BEARS	John Irving	£4.99
☐	99207 0	THE WATER METHOD MAN	John Irving	£4.99
☐	99205 4	THE WORLD ACCORDING TO GARP	John Irving	£6.99
☐	99141 4	PEEPING TOM	Howard Jacobson	£4.99
☐	99063 9	COMING FROM BEHIND	Howard Jacobson	£4.99
☐	99252 6	REDBACK	Howard Jacobson	£5.99